WORM
IN THE
BLOOD

Thomas Bloor

ff

faber and faber

First published in 2005
by Faber and Faber Limited
3 Queen Square London WC1N 3AU

Typeset by Faber and Faber Limited
Printed in England by Mackays of Chatham plc, Chatham, Kent

The right of Thomas Bloor
to be identified as author of this work has been
asserted in accordance with Section 77 of the Copyright,
Designs and Patents Act 1988

A CIP record for this book
is available from the British Library

ISBN 978–0–571–22595–8
ISBN 0–571–22595–0

2 4 6 8 10 9 7 5 3

Many thanks to Kathi, for her advice on horses.
Thanks also to Sue, and to Carole and Glenn.

In memory of
Patricia Jane Bloor (1956–2003)
who once gave me a dragon for dragons

I

Blood, Skin & Water

THE MARSH WAITS

It is past two o'clock in the morning. Out on the marshes, a shroud of mist hangs over the waterlogged ground. Thin tendrils of vapour ghost across the greasy surface of the old canal.

A fat rat, up on the towpath, freezes, and turns its head nervously towards the water. On the embankment, a dog fox, trotting over the railway sleepers, stops in his tracks and stares.

But there's nothing there. Not yet.

MEN OF HARLECH

'Oh go on, then! Let's hear it! Let's hear you defend this stinking hole we're living in!' Llew's forehead was beaded with sweat and his eyes were open wide.

'Dad! Listen, I never said –'

'I'm sick of hearing about how fantastic it is here. About your wonderful English friends!'

Sam took a deep breath. Drunk, he thought.

'Look, I didn't say that, it's just –'

Just that Sam had found Llew asleep in his wheel-chair with the back gas ring roaring and the kettle boiled dry. Drunk in charge of a cooker. There should be a law against it. But Llew was droning on, attack his only means of defence.

'And your marvellous English school! How you love it so much here, in this filthy city!'

Sam took another deep breath but the acrid smell from the burnt-out kettle filled his nostrils. Something snapped.

'Dad – shut up!'

There was silence. Llew looked up at Sam.

'If I wasn't in this chair, son,' Llew muttered, his voice low and throbbing with self-pity, 'you wouldn't be telling your own dad to shut up, I can tell you that.'

Sam glared at his father.

'If you hate it here so much why don't you just clear off back to Wales?'

Llew was silent for a while. He sat in his wheelchair and turned his head away.

'I couldn't do that, Sam,' he said at last. He spoke quietly now, seriously. 'I don't belong there no more. I wouldn't fit in, see? They'd come down hard on me if I went back to the valley. They'd push my wheelchair down Mynnodd Cairn, with me still in it. They'd set my hair alight first, too. Just for the look of it, see? They can be terrible unforgiving in the valley.'

Sam looked at his father.

'You're not serious,' he said.

'What do you think?' said Llew. He grasped the wheels of his chair and manoeuvred himself out into the kitchen.

Sam stood still, taking deep breaths, waiting for his anger to subside. He heard Llew clattering the pots and pans in the kitchen, whistling *Men of Harlech*.

It was just the two of them, living in the flat. They argued more and more these days. But Llew always seemed to get over their rows a lot quicker than Sam did. This was just one of the many ways in which Sam felt he was different from his father.

Llew liked to watch racing on TV. Grand National, Formula One or Olympics, he didn't care, so long as someone was going to win and a bunch of others were going to lose. He had run the London marathon a year before his accident, and had always been in the thick of things on the volleyball court, when he was in the Fire Service. He used to drive, too fast and too recklessly and with too much beer in his belly, even in the specially adapted car he used after losing the ability to walk. He was currently eighteen months into a three-year driving ban.

Sam, however, although he wasn't especially bad at sport, had no great love of it. He harboured a particular dislike of athletics. He wasn't interested in cars or driving. He didn't even ride a bike.

Llew had always been quick tempered. Sam, formerly a sulker by nature, now found himself snapping back more and more often. A niggling fear whispered at the back of his mind telling him that he was turning into his father.

Being angry with Llew led Sam, inevitably, to thoughts of his mother. She was dead, had been for years, but that never stopped him from comparing his parents, from contemplating the contrast between fragrant childhood memories of his mother and the whisky-reeking physical reality of his dad. It was a comparison he preferred not to make, and as his breathing slowed Sam closed his eyes and shook his head violently from side to side. This was one method he had of trying to stop thinking about his mother. But, as usual, it didn't work.

BROKEN GLASS

Twenty-five years earlier . . .

Suzie Lim placed the record on the turntable and flipped the needle down. She sat at her cluttered dressing table and a shiver of anticipation ran down her spine as she waited for the opening bars of the song. A little hiss and a crackle of vinyl, then here it came: the trembling, itching, sugary rhythm bounced out of the speakers and filled the bedroom. *Heart of Glass* – her favourite song.

She looked at herself in the mirror. Well, she was never going to be a blonde-haired, blue-eyed pop goddess like the woman in *Blondie*, she thought, but she knew the black make-up suited the shape of her eyes. She let the eyeliner run on beyond her upper eyelid, and turned the line up in an Ancient Egyptian style flourish, like the punk girls who hung out by the bus shelter on Market Street. Of course she wouldn't have dared to let her father see her like that, but it was fun to find out how she might have looked if she'd been born into a less traditional Luhngdonese family.

Down in the restaurant kitchen, Suzie's grandmother let out a grunt as she lifted the drum-sized tin of cooking oil. She struggled out of the kitchen and up the stairs, stopping halfway to get her breath back and secure a firmer grip on the heavy drum.

She could feel the touch of her son's silver cigarette lighter, pressed against her hip. She had tucked it into the waistband of her skirt. She knew what she had to do. She was going to burn the house down with everyone in it. It would be worth it.

Her son had thought that running away to England would free them, but the old woman knew he was wrong. They had brought it with them. The curse of Luhngdou. It was in their very blood. Only fire could cleanse them. Only in death could they find hope of redemption. This she knew. She had been taught it all her life.

The old woman had reached the top of the stairs now, and she stood on the landing outside her grand-daughter's door. Of all of them, it was most important that Suzie should burn. The young were the most ignorant, the most dangerous.

There was no need for silence. The thudding of the Western pop music Suzie listened to when her father was busy in the restaurant meant that the girl would hear no warning sounds from outside her door. The old woman unscrewed the cap and upturned the drum. Oil gushed out and spread into a thick pool.

She took the cigarette lighter from the band of her skirt. How could her granddaughter listen to those rubbishy pop songs? They all sounded the same. With a shaking hand, the old women flicked open the cap of the lighter. The flame flickered like a serpent's tongue tasting the air, blue at the base and orange at the tip.

She felt her knees click as she knelt down. I am too old, she thought. It will be a relief to be gone. And the girl too, if she knew what she really was, would not want their shame to continue, her grandmother was sure of it.

The last trace of the curse was about to be burnt out. And it had fallen to her to light the fire. It was a great honour. Reverently, she touched the flame to the oil.

But Suzie didn't die. Not then, anyway. It was another sixteen years before she died; from a heart condition that no one knew she had.

'*Heart of Glass!*' her widowed husband Llew Evans said, after the funeral. 'That was always her favourite song! And she never knew how fragile her own heart really was!' And then he span the wheels on his chair, whisky bottle in hand, and tried to tell anyone who'd listen a story they all knew already. With tears in his eyes, he told how he'd saved Suzie Lim from her blazing bedroom above the Green Dragon Chinese restaurant, back when he was a young fireman, and she was a girl of just eighteen, still half-way through her A-levels. He told how he loved her, and how he'd combined his name with hers on their wedding day, and that until the day he died he would always be Llywelyn Lim-Evans

WHITE HART

East London — 31 days ago.

A small man of oriental appearance, a priest, dressed in a black suit with a white dog collar, pushes open the frosted glass door and walks into the White Hart Inn. A pall of cigarette smoke hangs over everything, giving a misted blue tinge to the dimly lit interior. The cloying smell of stale sweat, and the mouldering sweetness of alcohol-soaked carpets, mingles with the tobacco smoke in the fetid air. The priest's nostrils twitch, once, but he gives no other sign of disquiet as he walks to the bar.

Silence falls. There are very few people in the White Hart tonight, but those that are have clearly been drinking for some time. The shelf by the pool table in the corner is stacked with empty glasses and beer bottles. Half a dozen men around the table all turn and stare as the priest makes his way across the room.

Although this is London, the most culturally mixed city in the UK, all the people in this particular pub are white. This is a run-down area called Iron Island, a sprawl of concrete car parks and high rise estates, built on a bend in the river to the east of the city.

'Good evening, gentlemen,' says the priest, 'my name is Father David Lee.'

'You can't come in here,' says a man in a brown leather coat. He sags over the bar, a lager bottle in his hand.

'But I am in here,' says Father David, smiling.

Brown Leather turns on his bar stool.

'No. You don't understand. You' — he points a wavering finger at the small priest — 'cannot — come — in — here.'

Father David shrugs, still smiling. He watches as the men around the pool table leave their game and begin drifting over to the bar.

'Skinner,' Brown Leather says, 'I think we need to see your tattoo.'

The one called Skinner drains his glass but keeps hold of the empty pint pot. He walks forward with the rolling gait of a man who, for whatever reason, appears unable, or unwilling, to fully close his legs. His companions also move in, forming a loose circle around the little priest, cutting off his retreat route. They grip their pool cues by the thin end, holding them like baseball bats, like clubs. None of them look too steady on their feet, but the drink has also made them aggressive. Here is a stranger, an oriental. And these men are racists. They make no bones about it.

Skinner looks at the man in brown leather, perched on the tall bar stool. Brown Leather gives him a nod so Skinner lifts his tee shirt and reveals a large tattoo of a Union Jack flag, right across his belly.

Brown Leather points at Skinner's tattoo.

'You know what that is?' he says.

'A man's stomach?' says the priest.

No one laughs. No one smiles.

'It's the flag of this country,' says Brown Leather. 'Our country. You'll notice that there're only three colours in it. Red. White. Blue. There ain't no yellow in it. Never has been. Never will be.'

At that moment the door of the pub bangs open. The men all look round sharply, all except the little oriental priest.

A middle-aged woman, thin as a crab apple tree, with a head of coarse grey hair, clatters into the pub, carrying two large suitcases.

'Oh! Father David! There you are!' she says. 'Whatever's going on?'

'I was hoping to ask these gentlemen for directions, Mrs Hare,' says the priest. 'But instead they are giving me a most interesting illustrated talk on the flag of the United Kingdom.'

'Really?' says Mrs Hare. She straightens the thick-rimmed spectacles she wears and looks over at the men.

'Yes,' Father David continues. 'I am looking forward to the next part of this entertainment, where Mr Skinner here will doubtless animate the Union flag, giving it the appearance of fluttering in the breeze, by the artful rippling of his stomach muscles.' The priest smiles at the circle of blank-faced men. 'Am I right, gentlemen?'

Brown Leather stands up. His face is white with fury. 'This is no joke!' he says, spitting as he speaks.

'You' – he jabs a finger at Father David – 'need - to be taught - a lesson. Get hold of him!'

The circle closes. The priest's arms are pinioned behind his back. Skinner smashes his beer glass on the edge of the bar and holds a jagged shard to Father David's throat.

'Please,' the priest says. He talks quietly, carefully. The razor-sharp glass presses into the skin on his neck as he speaks. 'I really must advise you to let me go. I do not wish you to come to any harm.'

'*You* don't want *us* to be harmed?' Brown Leather says. 'Oh, wait a minute. I get it. You want us to think you're some kind of martial arts expert, don't you? A deadly Kung Fu assassin or whatever. Well, I've got news for you, priest! We're not scared of yellow-skinned vicars round here, even if you can do karate.'

'It is not I you have reason to fear,' Father David says. 'It is her.' His eyes flicker towards the door. The two suitcases stand there side by side, but of Mrs Hare there is now no sign.

A sudden whirring sound fills the air, the sort of noise a branch makes when it's whipped back and forth by a raging gale. Then there's a crack, a thud, and a snapping noise, like a green twig being twisted and bent. There are some muffled screams and moans.

Brown Leather looks around him, wildly. His gang of thugs are all lying strewn about the floor.

'What?' he says. 'What?' A sweat born of panic has broken out on his forehead. He swings out with his fist as a shadow moves behind him, but he doesn't even see his attacker, let alone connect.

A foot crunches into his jaw, knocking his head down, hard, against the corner of the bar. He clatters to the floor. The last thing he sees, before he slips into the dark fog of unconsciousness, is a grey-haired woman in an anorak standing over him, one leg raised in the air. The thick-rimmed glasses have slipped down her nose. With one finger, she pushes them back into place.

'That will do, Mrs Hare,' says Father David. 'We can ask for directions elsewhere.'

UNDER THE FLYOVER

Georgette was happy. She was on Dandelion and she didn't have to think about anything else. She rode the horse around and around the indoor arena while over her head the motorway thundered and roared. She liked to imagine the drivers, in their lorries and their vans and their cars, gritting their teeth and gripping the steering wheel as they rode the flyover, none of them knowing that beneath their wheels, beneath the cold grey tarmac, there was a girl called Georgette riding a horse called Dandelion.

Sometimes the girl spoke to the horse, but naturally enough, the horse never replied. Georgette didn't mind. No one spoke to her all that much, not here, at the stables, not at home, not at school. No one except the new girl.

Georgette wondered why Adda-Leigh spoke to her. Was it an attempt to draw her out of her shell, like the denim mini-skirt and black nail varnish, neither of which she ever wore, that her mother had given her for Christmas? But no, that couldn't be it. Adda-Leigh spoke to everyone. She spoke to Leticia and she spoke to Michael Taranti, and they were both very scary people. She spoke to Molly K, who once wore the same jumper, with the same ketchup stains down the front, without ever getting it washed throughout an entire term. She spoke to Ursula, who helped out in the library at lunchtime and played the cello in the school orchestra. She spoke to that weird half-Chinese boy, Sam, with the odd-looking hair. She even spoke to the teachers. The new girl clearly wasn't fussy, Georgette concluded. That was why Adda-Leigh spoke to her.

But now the horse rider frowned. She had allowed both her school and her mother to float into her thoughts and contaminate the mindless pleasure of riding. Another letter had come this morning. She hadn't opened it but she knew it would be full of hints about how much the twins would love to see her and how lovely the countryside was up north and have you got a boyfriend yet and, as usual, no mention of her father at all. She didn't care how much the twins wanted to see her, she didn't want to see them. They weren't even related to her, just her mother's boyfriend's children, why would she want to see them?

Georgette didn't want to live up north. She wanted to stay living with her dad, in London, to stay lost forever in the anonymity of the crowd. She'd managed to slip through the cracks, to drop out of sight. These days she could move through school unnoticed and unchallenged, alone and secure within the limited confines of her own company. But now the new girl had started talking to her.

Sensing his rider's distractedness, Dandelion slowed to a walk. Georgette pulled on the reins and brought the horse to a halt. She swung herself out of the saddle then slid down Dandelion's flank and onto the sand-covered ground. Next time, she would take the horse out onto the marsh, no matter how waterlogged the ground was. It was easier not to think in the open air.

Another forty-five minutes had passed before she was ready to leave the stables. She had to lead Dandelion back to his stall, pick out his hooves and fork in some fresh straw bedding. Then she had to return the saddle and bridle to the tack room, where, in the dim light of a single naked bulb, she sprayed the cherry-red leather with Higginbottom's Equestrian Tackle Shampoo and wiped it over with a damp sponge. All this Georgette achieved in a blissful state of vacancy. But her peace of mind was not to last.

She saw him as she walked across the small outdoor paddock, towards the gate. He was out there on the marsh, just beyond the fence. Sam Lim-Evans from school.

Sam was running. Not jogging or long-distance or football-training-type running. This looked more like blind panic. More like headlong flight.

Lance, the stable's belligerent Alsatian guard dog, had left his wooden kennel and was at the full extent of his chain, staring at the running youth with hackles raised. Georgette gave the dog a wide berth. She expected to hear him growl or bark. Instead he let out a stifled whimper.

Lance was vicious. Even chained up he was frightening. He caught rats and killed them with a single shake of his muzzle. But now, looking through the wire mesh fence at Sam running by, the guard dog had his tail between his legs and was shivering. The raised hair on his shoulders had collapsed and he slunk back into the darkness of his wooden shelter with a jangle of chain links and a low canine moan.

Out on the marsh, Sam seemed to echo the Alsatian's distress with a wordless cry of his own, a painful and desolate yelp, dragged from the back of his throat. With that, he ploughed full tilt into a waterlogged tyre rut, sending up a great wall of spray. Holding his head in his hands, he fell to his knees in the muddy water.

Standing, frozen, halfway across the paddock, Georgette looked out at him through the wire.

THE HOT AND THE COLD

Sam felt the water trickling over his face. It ran into his eyes and down his cheeks. He felt the chill slickness of the wet mud beneath his calves. Icy marsh water slopped against his midriff. It was all a blessed relief.

This was the worst he'd ever felt it. The burning sensation that flickered over his skin and smouldered deep in his bones was tormenting him again. The attacks were becoming more frequent. They often followed arguments with his father, as if the rage that swept through him on those occasions actually kindled some kind of conflagration within his biology. He felt like a building on fire.

'Hello!' A girl's voice, someone not used to calling out, an unwilling voice. 'Sam! Do you need any help?'

Sam turned his head. He saw her standing at the

fence, peering through the wire, looking at him. A girl from school. That small girl, short, thin, sort of wizened-looking despite being no more than fourteen. She reminded Sam of one of the cactus plants his dad bought and then neglected, left lined up along the window ledge in the living room covered in dust and cactus-blight. Georgette.

The burning seemed to have subsided. He wondered how long she had been watching him. He stared at her and shook his head, slowly.

'No!' he shouted. His voice sounded unexpectedly harsh.

A look passed over her features. Sam realised, with a mild sense of hurt, that it was a look of relief. He watched as Georgette hurried away, over to the iron-bar gate, which she shut behind her, carefully. She disappeared along the track that led to the street.

Back home, standing outside the flat, Sam found his fingers were completely numb with the cold and damp. Pulling the keys from the pocket of his sodden jeans had been difficult enough. Now, as he tried to turn the key in the lock, his thumb and forefinger refused to work together. His thumb just bent limply at the knuckle and his fingers slipped and fumbled uselessly. The key could not be turned.

'Oh my days! What happened to you?'

Before he could turn, footsteps clacked up behind him and the new girl, Adda-Leigh, was looking him up and down.

'Did you fall in a pond?' she asked, smiling broadly. 'Or did somebody chuck you in?'

This was typical Adda-Leigh. She brimmed with easy self-confidence and already seemed quite at home both at school and on the streets of her new neighbourhood.

Sam coughed. 'I've been over the marsh.'

Adda-Leigh puzzled him. She was stylish and pretty, not the sort of girl he would expect to find engaging him in conversation. And yet she'd made a point of saying hello to him in Humanities the other day, and now here she was again.

'The marsh?' Adda-Leigh's eyes widened. 'That's dirty water over there, boy!' she said to him. 'You want to watch you don't catch something nasty. There's rats there, down on the canal. They all wee in the water. That's how you get Weil's disease, you know. You'll think you've got the flu, but Weil's is much worse. You go to bed and in the morning you're not alive no more.' She snapped her fingers. 'The rat's wee gets into your blood. You got any paper cuts?' She took hold of both his hands, to inspect them for cuts, but snatched her fingers away as if she had been burnt.

'Your hands are like ice, boy!'

Sam looked at her dumbly. She had skin like polished wood. Her eyes were almost black, like Indian ink. He didn't want to try the lock again, not until she'd gone. He felt foolish, standing there in his sopping wet clothes, unable to get into his own flat. But Adda-Leigh didn't seem to be in any hurry.

'This your house?'

'Flat,' said Sam.

'Whatever. Can't you get in? Are those the wrong keys or something? Here, let me try.'

The keys were still in the lock. She moved past him, reached out her hand and turned the key. The door swung open.

'You should get some dry clothes on,' she said, turning away. 'And don't forget Weil's disease. Check for cuts. If you wake up dead in the morning, don't say I didn't warn you!' She waved from the front gate. 'Otherwise, I'll see you in school tomorrow. Bye!'

She walked off down the road, her beaded hair extensions bobbing on her shoulders. She didn't look back. Sam watched her go, standing by the open door to the flat.

SCRATCHED

Sam had a bath. He lay back in the steam and hot water and closed his eyes. The edge of the enamel tub pressed hard against the back of his head.

When the water got a little cold, Sam leant forward and turned the hot tap on. He lay back and scratched his arm, just at the bend of the elbow.

'Sam!' Llew hammered on the bathroom door. 'Don't use up all the hot!'

Steaming water gushed onto Sam's toes. He shifted his legs. Bath water slopped over the edge of the tub.

He heard the wheels of Llew's chair squeaking on the lino in the hall. The hammering came again. 'And don't get the floor all soaking, Sammy! You messy little git!'

Sam raised his foot and turned off the tap with his toe.

Lying back in the soapy water, he scratched his arm again. He noticed a patch of blotchy red skin, the size of a fifty pence piece, on the inner joint of his elbow. He looked closer. A rash.

Was it something he'd caught over on the marsh? He thought of Adda-Leigh's rats. He pictured a line of rodents standing on their hindquarters on the towpath, all peeing in the canal.

He stared at the rash on his arm. A microbe in the dirty marsh water had penetrated the skin on his elbow. He had contracted a disease, some kind of dermatitis.

He looked closer. The skin was blistered and the itching was growing in intensity, as if just looking at it was causing the irritation to build and swell to a maddening crescendo. This was an itch that demanded his attention. It was insisting that it be scratched and it would brook no refusal. Sam gave in, and scratched the rash long and hard.

BLOOD AND ICE CREAM

Central London — 28 days ago.

No one in Chinatown will tell Father David anything. He is fluent in several Chinese dialects but it does him no good. His mother tongue is Luhngdonese, and no one speaks that language here. Something in his use of words, some trace of an accent, betrays his origin and puts people on their guard. No one will admit to knowing anyone from Luhngdou, or hearing of anyone from that island ever settling in the UK.

There are many strange stories about Luhngdou, but who would tell such tales here, amidst the bright midday bustle of the shops and restaurants? People from Luhngdou have been known to disappear suddenly. Or meet with accidents. No one wants any trouble. No one knows anything.

Father David and Mrs Hare had flown into London City Airport three days ago, caught the wrong bus, wandered like lost souls around Iron Island, encountered a little local difficulty, and eventually found their way to a hotel near the British Museum. They have scoured the noodle bars, restaurants and oriental gift shops of Soho and Covent Garden. They are looking for someone.

But no one knows anything.

In Leicester Square, heading for the Tube, the priest and his grey-haired companion struggle through the heaving crowds of tourists. A man in a yellow baseball hat jostles Father David, slams into him, then apologises, patting the little priest on the shoulder and on the back before moving away into the crowd.

'I'm surprised he even apologised!' Mrs Hare pushes her glasses back onto the bridge of her nose. 'People here are just so rude!'

Father David looks up at Mrs Hare. He feels for his wallet.

'My pocket's been picked.'

Mrs Hare's eyes widen. Her pink, outdoor cheeks redden a little and a shadow crosses her brow.

'Right,' she says. 'I shan't be a moment.'

'Mrs Hare!' Father David calls out to her retreating back. She is forcing her way through the crowd with relentless purpose, heading after the man in the yellow hat. 'Mrs Hare! Gently, if you please!'

He wants to tell her to stop, to leave the thief alone, but he knows the loss of his money and contact addresses would seriously affect their mission. If their search failed, the consequences could reach far beyond the fate of a single London pick-pocket. Nevertheless, it's not for the first time that he wonders how he, a priest, a believer in the ways of peace, in turning the other cheek, ended up in partnership with a being such as Mrs Hare.

Father David shudders, and heads for a nearby ice-cream parlour.

A surly waitress takes his order.

'A chocolate fudge sundae with candy scatterings, topped with double cream and fresh cherries, please. And a small vanilla ice. No wafer. Thank you.'

Mrs Hare arrives just as the ice creams are brought to the table.

'Splendid!' she wheezes, slightly out of breath. Father David raises his eyebrows.

'No, no. No difficulties.' She places his wallet on the table and beams at him. 'I caught up with him in an alleyway off Charing Cross Road.'

As she adjusts her glasses, Father David cannot help but notice the fresh bloodstains on her sleeve.

IN THE DEAD OF NIGHT

Sam felt the wind streaming over the goose-pimpled flesh of his upper body. The cold air felt good on his arm, where the rash burned and throbbed and itched furiously.

But something was wrong. Very wrong.

Shouldn't he be in bed, lying down, horizontal, with a pillow under his head and a mattress beneath him? He shouldn't be upright, with his hands clasped around cold iron rungs and his legs, from the knee down, submerged in icy water. The only sounds should be the quiet ticking of his alarm clock and his father's muffled snoring from the next room. The air should not be filled by the slop of water and the creak of tree branches shifting in the wind.

Sam opened his eyes. A blank concrete wall was

before him. He was holding onto the rungs of an iron ladder, set into concrete. The wall was not a wall, he realised. It was the side of the canal. He had climbed down a rusted iron ladder leading to the dark water. His legs were already half submerged.

A wave of dizziness swept over him. Utterly disorientated, he felt his fingers relax their grip on the rungs. He was about to slip into the freezing, slow-moving water, where he would drown. And he would never even know what he was doing there.

A shout of horror broke from his lips and he was suddenly wide-awake, his heart in his mouth. This is no dream, he thought, dragging himself up the ladder and out of the canal, scrambling onto the towpath. This is real.

His pyjama bottoms were soaked, but at least he was wearing some. His top half was naked to the elements and he was feeling extremely chilled. Hunched over and with his hands clasped in front of his chest, he stumbled along the towpath until he reached the row of concrete bollards at the end of Mire Street. He padded up the middle of the road, his bare feet seeking out the relative smoothness of the road markings, the white lines, which seemed to be leading him home. He turned the corner into Dartmead Lane and there was the flat, the front door half open, and behind it, darkness.

He had seen no one. No lights burned in the windows of the houses he passed. The clouds were blowing across the moon, but otherwise all was still, all was quiet.

Sam slipped into the flat and closed the door behind him, quietly. He let out a long sigh and looked at his reflection in the hall mirror. He stared, trying to find some clue in his own features to explain what had just happened to him.

He gave up and headed for his bedroom. The light flicked on in the kitchen as he approached the open door. Sam froze, the hair prickling at the back of his neck.

'Who is it?' he called out. His voice sounded jagged and hoarse.

'Who do you think?'

Llew was sitting in his wheelchair, blinking. He wore a large white vest. A blanket covered his legs. There was a half-eaten sandwich on a plate, balanced on his lap.

'Couldn't sleep, see? Must have dozed off out here,' he said. He picked up the sandwich. 'You all right, son? You having trouble sleeping too?'

Sam nodded.

'What's that on your arm?' said Llew, through a mouthful of bread and cheese.

'Nothing.' Sam wrapped his fingers around his

elbow, covering up the rash. To Llew, a nasty skin complaint could provide ammunition for countless jibes at Sam's expense. He didn't always seem to know the difference between humour and humiliation. Sam moved past the kitchen door and into the soft darkness of his room.

The alarm woke him a few hours later. Numb with fatigue and with the sour tang of the canal water still clinging to him, he stumbled out into the bathroom and opened the medicine cabinet. At the back of the cupboard he found a dusty packet labelled CREPE BANDAGE.

He wound the bandage around his arm, covering the rash, which was bigger now, the size of a five-pound note, spreading down along the inside of his forearm. He fastened the bandage with a piece of sticking plaster. His skin seemed to squirm and pulse beneath the tight-wound cotton.

SHIRTS VERSUS SKINS

Mr Slough wore a red tracksuit. A whistle was slung round his neck on a length of nylon cord. Sam wore a striped rugby shirt, the sleeves of which barely reached halfway down to his wrists, above a pair of billowing cotton shorts that had long since faded from their original black to a weary-looking grey-green.

He had forgotten his games kit.

'Forgotten your kit?' Mr Slough had eyed him, glassily. 'Right. Detention tomorrow night. Now you can go through the lost property box in my office and get yourself something to wear this lesson. You don't get out of it that easy.'

The rugby shirt was several sizes too small. The tight sleeve tugged at Sam's bandaged elbow as he pushed his arm through it.

'What happened to you?' Aaron had seen the bandage. He was sitting on the bench next to Sam, leaning
forward, slowly doing up the laces on his trainers with
his awkward, puffy fingers. Everyone else had already
gone into the gym.

'It's nothing. It's just a thing,' Sam said.

'You two boys! Get a move on! Now!' Mr Slough's
voice rang through the changing rooms.

The rest of the class were bouncing basketballs in
the gym. The sound rang around the iron rafters and
echoed off the walls, a chaos of percussive slapping.
Today the noise seemed to penetrate Sam's skull with
more force than usual.

Mr Slough's whistle shrilled. The ball-bouncing
frenzy petered out.

'Who got all these balls out?' Mr Slough said mildly.
To the uninitiated, it might have sounded like a casual,
almost friendly enquiry. No one answered. The boys
knew what was coming.

Mr Slough picked up a basketball that had come to
rest near his foot.

'We are playing basketball,' he said, his voice rising
suddenly to a shout. '*And if we're playing basketball —*'
He slammed the ball down onto the polished wooden
floor of the gym. It made a high-pitched pneumatic
ringing sound as it rebounded twenty feet in the air.
Mr Slough's voice now rose from a shout to a furious

bellow. 'IF WE'RE PLAYING BASKETBALL WE ONLY NEED ONE BALL!' Mr Slough caught the basketball as it came down and glared around the gym.

Sam wondered what the girls were doing out on the field. Hockey, he supposed. It was a raw and overcast day, but even so he felt a pang of envy. The rash throbbed and itched under its bandage and, with the tight shirtsleeve encasing it, he could barely bend his arm at all. His head, too, was beginning to pound. To be outside, out in the air, would have been infinitely better than this.

The spare basketballs were put away and the class divided into teams.

'Right.' Mr Slough turned to Sam's team. 'You lot can go skins.'

'Going skins' meant that the designated team had to remove their tops, to distinguish them from their shirted opponents. Sam sighed. Getting the minuscule shirt on had been hard enough, now he had to take it off again. There was a lump in his throat. His tongue felt thick and slow, filling up his mouth. The urge to tell Mr Slough precisely what he could do with his referee's whistle was suddenly very strong, but he didn't feel as if he could form the words. With a sensation of growing panic he found himself stepping forward. What was happening to him? He never challenged his teachers, it just wasn't his style. There wasn't even any good reason to be getting so het up.

Sam forced himself to step back into the crowd of now shirtless boys, but there was still a choking tightness in his chest and it wasn't the shirt that was causing it. He realised he was getting angry. Very angry.

BULLY OFF

Georgette shivered and looked up at the dark grey clouds. It had begun to spit with rain.

A seagull hung on the keen wind that blew across the playing field. The bird seemed utterly motionless, suspended in the air. Here was a creature perfectly in tune with its physical abilities and with the world around it.

Someone screamed out 'Georgette!' and she felt an agonising blow as the hockey ball hammered into her shin. Leticia was glaring at her.

'Sorry.' Georgette mumbled the word, automatically.

The ball trickled out of play. Georgette was left wondering why hockey balls were made out of concrete. Leticia jogged past and caught her on the back of the knee with her stick, knocking her to the ground.

Georgette said nothing. She tried to keep herself away from the hub of the action, to remain peripheral, unnoticed, invisible.

'Don't hide your light under a bushel, Georgette!' her mother had said to her on a crackly phone line the last time she'd spoken to her. 'Make the most of yourself. You're young! Time for you to shine!'

Georgette had said nothing.

'Hello? Georgie? You still there?'

Georgette didn't want to shine. She wanted to hide. Particularly in PE lessons.

Adda-Leigh, on the other hand, had a very different approach, one that Georgette, in spite of herself, couldn't help but admire.

Adda-Leigh seemed to enjoy PE immensely, but not in the way girls like Leticia did. Instead of shouting at her team mates, attempting to injure her opponents and sulking furiously at every reversal on the field of play, Adda-Leigh's approach was different. It was as if she wasn't running around a muddy field in the freezing cold at all. She behaved more as if she was dancing the night away in some luxurious nightclub. She would laugh or whoop with pleasure as she dodged down the centre of the pitch and struck the ball sweetly into the corner of the goal. When playing hockey, she shimmied, she glided, and she pirouetted, all with a serene grin on her face that drove Leticia mad. Above all else, she refused to take the game seriously, never took any account of the score, and displayed complete indifference to any impact her performance might have on the outcome of the match. Georgette could see that she wasn't much of a team player. But then, neither was Georgette.

Leticia had just scored with a brutal shot from point blank range and Adda-Leigh was trotting to the centre of the pitch now, to bully off. She pointed to Georgette and turned to the teacher.

'Miss! Georgette's leg's bleeding!'

Georgette looked down, surprised. Her knee was oozing blood. She must have landed on a particularly hard piece of ground when Leticia knocked her down, but was too numb with cold to feel much pain.

'She needs a plaster from the office, Miss! I'll go with her!' Adda-Leigh took Georgette by the arm. 'Come on, girl, let's go.'

They heard the shouting as they walked round the side of the gym. It was coming from inside. The boy's PE teacher was bawling at someone again.

'Get out, get changed and go to the duty room!' They heard every bellowed word through the gymnasium walls.

Adda-Leigh pulled a face.

'That Mr Slough needs to watch his blood pressure! We had a teacher at my old school, he was always screaming at us. One day, at break time, he was getting all aggravated with some kid he'd kept back after the lesson, when suddenly he claps a hand to his chest. He starts gasping and wheezing and looking all desperate, his lips go blue and he slumps down over his desk.

Then the bell went.

The kid he'd been barking at was a bit dim so he just goes off to his next lesson and doesn't say nothing about what had happened. The next class come in, but they thought the teacher had fallen asleep and they were too scared to wake him up. This went on all day. Ambulance didn't come for him till four o'clock!'

'Was he dead?'

'Yep. As a dodo!'

'You made that up!'

They were crossing the playground in front of the gym. Adda-Leigh opened her mouth to respond, but at that point the doors were pushed open violently and Sam came bursting out. He was wearing nothing but his trainers and a pair of enormous shorts. A bandage, wound round one arm, had come loose and was trailing behind him as he ran, fluttering like the tail of a kite.

Sam clearly had no intention of going to the duty

room. He ran straight to the school gates and away down the road. Mr Slough appeared, red-faced, at the door to the gym. He let out a shrill burst on his whistle, but Sam did not slow, not even for a moment.

Now it was Georgette's turn to pull a face.

'It was that Sam.'

'You don't like him?' Adda-Leigh arched her eyebrows.

'Yuk! No! I think he's mental or something. I saw him over the marsh the other day, jumping in the puddles. He's not right in the head.'

But Adda-Leigh was gazing after Sam as he sped away down the road.

'I like his skin,' she said. 'Looks like he's made out of gold.'

UP FROM THE UNDERGROUND

Waterloo Station, London — 25 days ago.

Mrs Hare drags both suitcases up the stairs. Father David rides the escalator.

'Beat you!' says Mrs Hare, panting, red-faced, waiting for him on the tiled platform concourse at the top of the stairs.

'Come on, this way!' She sets off through the crowds that throng the concourse, milling around the station shops and cafés and stalls.

Father David eyes the departure board, anxiously.

'There!' he says, pointing up at the board. 'Twelve-seventeen to Milford Haven.'

'I know, I know, Platform Six.' Mrs Hare hops excitedly from foot to foot, and pushes the spectacles back up the bridge of her nose. 'Welsh Wales here we come!'

Father David shakes his head as he follows Mrs Hare, who is dodging through the crowds with a suit-case in each hand.

He sighs, and reminds himself that they're following the only clue they've found. Someone who knew someone who remembered someone who had once mentioned hearing of a Luhngdonese family that owned a restaurant in Wales.

'I only hope we're not wasting our time, Mrs Hare,' he says, more to himself than to his companion. She's too far ahead to hear him, in any case.

MYSTERIOUS WAYS

Sam felt it first when Mickey Taranti slapped him on the back. There, on his shoulder blade. The same throbbing, squirming, insistent itch. The rash was multiplying.

Michael Taranti, hard man of Year Nine, feared throughout the lower school, known to the Year Sevens as 'The Dreaded Enforcer', that same Taranti who, to the best of Sam's knowledge, had never said a word to him in the three years they'd spent as form mates, Mickey now strode past him and slapped him on the back.

It was the day after the incident with the basketball in the gymnasium.

'Didn't know you had it in you, mate!' he said, with a grin like a crocodile. Then he was away, into the streams of kids that were flooding in through the gates.

'Did you hear what happened? It was unbelievable!' Aaron was by the main entrance, waving his arms around, drawing a crowd about him to listen to the story once again. 'Sam Lim-Evans, right?' He pointed him out to a knot of wide-eyed Year Sevens. 'That heroic youth creeping into school over there. Sam, right? Don't be fooled by appearances because he, that insignificant looking kid there, took on Slough, on his own turf, and lived to tell the tale.'

'What'd he do?' someone asked.

'Don't you know? You must be the very last kid left in the school that doesn't know!' Aaron was milking it, playing to the crowd. But then the bell went for morning registration and his audience started to drift away. He had to cut the story short.

'You want to know what he did? He only went and bounced a basketball off old Slough's nose, didn't he? Flung it right at him. Hard.'

'What! How come he's still in school? I'd have thought they'd suspend him for that!'

'Yeah. Suspend him by his you-know-whats if Slough had anything to do with it! But no. They have shown mercy. The Head moves in mysterious ways!'

Sam, walking into the main building, heard Aaron's lumbering jogtrot as he ran to catch him up.

Loose change jangled in his friend's pockets, his feet pounded the industrial lino of the school corridor and the books heaved and shifted in his backpack as he ran. Sam had noticed a high-pitched ringing in his ears today, but his hearing, in fact, felt remarkably sharp.

Aaron clapped a heavy hand on Sam's shoulder. Sam shook him off.

'Calm down!' Aaron fell into step beside him. 'I'm not Slough, you know! So' – now Aaron dropped his voice a little – 'what happened after you legged it out of school?'

Sam looked sideways at Aaron. 'What's the matter? Running out of juicy stories for your twenty-four-hour news service?'

'Don't be like that!' Aaron assumed a hurt expression.

They were nearly at their form room. Sam sighed. 'Okay. I went home. Dad was in. He phoned the school. He's coming in today for a meeting with the Head.'

Aaron winced. 'Nasty!'

'Yeah,' Sam nodded. 'And Aaron –'

Aaron turned.

'Yeah?'

'You were there. You saw what happened. You know I never meant to hit Slough with that ball, don't you?

Okay, I lost it, I totally lost it. But I never meant to hit him in the face.'

Now it was Aaron's turn to sigh.

'Yeah, I know,' he said. 'It doesn't make such a decent story if you tell it like that though, does it?'

Sam let Aaron move past him into the form room. Then he lifted one arm and reached around, elbow bent behind his head, to scratch vigorously at his itching shoulder blade before he followed Aaron in.

NOT SPEAKING

Llew wasn't speaking to Sam. He had taken a taxi to school for the meeting with the Head. That alone, Sam knew, would have put him in a bad mood.

For a start, he would have resented shelling out good money to go on such a miserable outing. And then there was all the hassle of getting in to and out of the cab, of sorting out the chair and avoiding the look of pity that Llew always expected to see in the driver's eye.

Then there was the meeting itself. Sam was pulled out of class to come and mumble an apology to a rather sheepish-looking Mr Slough. The Head grimly shook Sam's father by the hand and asked him if everything was 'all right at home'. It was the sort of situation that Llew found unbearable.

It was now four-thirty in the afternoon. Sam was in his room, sitting on the bed with his shirt off. The shaving mirror from the bathroom was held in one hand. He was trying to look at the rash on his shoulder blade. He twisted and turned, craned his neck, tried the mirror in one hand, then the other, but it was impossible to get the right angle.

He knew the rash was there. He could feel it. But he wanted to see if it looked the same as the skin on his arm.

He had taken off the bandage. The rash was bigger now, spreading from halfway up to his shoulder to halfway down to his wrist. The skin was red and covered with livid blisters, tingling with a combination of soreness and irritation. At the joint of his arm, where the rash had first flared up, the blisters had flaked and burst and the skin was peeling away to reveal a raw but surprisingly hard layer of mottled flesh beneath. It was strangely coloured, spotted, with tinges of blue and orange. It was this lurid coloration that alarmed Sam more than anything.

He threw down the mirror and closed his eyes. He rocked back and forward on the bed, with one hand covering his arm, so he didn't have to look at the discoloured skin. He chewed on his lip. What should he do?

Llew would be over his bad mood fairly soon, but

Sam didn't want to show his dad the rash. The man had no patience with other people's maladies. Sam never took a day off school, preferring to struggle on through colds and viral infections rather than put up with Llew's cold-eyed contempt if he stayed at home. Even the grazed knees and cut fingers Sam had suffered when he was in primary school had been greeted with a dismissive glance, or, at best, the careless application of a sticking plaster. So he wasn't going to show his dad the rash. He didn't want Llew poking at it, or pulling a face, or blaming him for it, or questioning his personal hygiene. He didn't want to tell Llew about going to the marsh, or sleepwalking in the canal. He just wanted the rash to clear up of its own accord. He just wanted to feel normal again.

But it didn't look like that was going to happen. The weird, discoloured skin seemed to suggest some kind of infection. And now the rash had sprung up on his shoulder blade, too. It had to be stopped. He needed help.

GUNPOWDER SURGERY

The surgery was up on Gunpowder Row. Sam hadn't been there for years. The last time he went to the doctor's he'd gone with his mother.

He remembered holding her hand as they walked to the end of Mire Street. They had ambled along, opposite the shops. The pace had been slow enough for him to stop and stroke a black cat, sitting on a wall, and then have no difficulty catching up with his mother. He knew now that she had only walked that slowly because, due to her heart condition, she was too short of breath to go any faster.

He had asked her for an iced doughnut from the baker's across the street. She'd said he could have one after she'd seen the doctor. Sam wondered how it was that he could remember details like these when the memory of his mother's face had already faded to almost nothing.

Now he walked along the same stretch of road and glanced across at the row of shops. The baker's had gone. Closed down. Sheets of corrugated steel had been bolted over the window where the cakes had once been displayed. Several layers of gaudy posters had been pasted over the tarnished steel. Their images and slogans, advertising last month's club night or previous new releases by obscure pop acts destined never to be heard of again, were all strangely distorted by the bend and dip of the corrugated surface.

The doctor's surgery was on the corner. The entrance looked very different to how Sam remembered it. A newly built extension had been added at the side of the building. Above the door was a new-looking sign that said GUNPOWDER SURGERY. Below it was another sign: RECEPTION.

Inside, a tall counter confronted Sam. Behind the counter there was a woman with a telephone held to her ear. Two other women were busily searching through the bundles of files that filled the shelving on the walls behind.

'No – I'm sorry – No – I'm afraid that's not possible.'

The receptionist was speaking into the phone but she seemed to be staring straight at Sam as she spoke.

There was a vacant smile on her lips. 'No. We can't offer repeat prescriptions over the phone –'

A long silence followed as the person on the phone presumably went into lengthy details about their health problems. The receptionist continued to smile as she listened. Every now and then she parted her lips to speak but was unable to interrupt the caller. But at last she managed it. 'No – I'm sorry, no – You'll have to come in to the surgery. Yes. You'll have to come in. Tomorrow morning? Eight-thirty. Goodbye.'

She replaced the telephone receiver, carefully, and now her eyes properly focused on Sam for the first time.

'Can I help you?'

'I need to see the doctor.'

'Have you got an appointment?' she reached for a ledger lying open on the counter.

'No . . . I . . .' Sam was thrown by this. 'I wanted to see the doctor.'

'Now? I'm sorry you can't see Doctor now. You have to make an appointment.' She pulled the book towards her and picked up a pen. 'How about Tuesday the twenty-ninth?'

'When?'

'Tuesday the twenty-ninth. Two weeks' time.'

'Two weeks!' Sam was appalled.

An old woman had shuffled into the surgery and

was standing in line behind him. She gave a wheezy cough.

'What doctor do you normally see?' The receptionist looked at Sam and raised her eyebrows, enquiringly.

This was another surprise.

'Doctor Simons.' As soon as he said the name Sam knew he was making a mistake. Doctor Simons had been old, he remembered. Very old. Stooped, wrinkled, balding, and what little hair he did have had been as white as snow. And that was eight years ago. He was probably retired by now. Or dead.

A young mother, carrying a toddler on her hip, joined the queue behind the old woman with the cough.

'I'm afraid we don't have a Doctor Simons. This is a group surgery. Are you registered here?'

Sam looked at the ground and hunched his shoulder. He felt his face redden. The heat beneath his skin was unbearable. He had to get out.

'I'll just go then,' he muttered, and he turned away.

'Pardon?' The receptionist's voice was very loud.

The old woman regarded Sam through rheumy eyes. The toddler stared at him, wide-eyed, as if Sam were an object of fear, or of wonder. The young mother turned her head and looked away.

Sam blundered past them and out into the street. The rash on his arm and on his back throbbed and squirmed and screamed out to be scratched. His face felt as though it would burst into flames at any moment. Just as uncontrollable anger had taken him over in the sports hall, now a feeling of acute embarrassment threatened to consume him utterly.

He crossed the road outside the surgery but misjudged the flow of traffic. A car horn blared and he had to scurry the last few yards to the safety of the pavement opposite. A motorist shouted out a single blunt obscenity as he sped past. Sam was in no doubt that it had been aimed at him.

He tripped on the curb and stumbled across the pavement. The old baker's shop was there in front of him. He came to a stop, breathing hard. Slowly, he leant forward and laid his forehead against the corrugated steel frontage. He closed his eyes. The metal sheeting felt cool and soothing, pressed against his burning skin.

THREE WORDS

Powys, Wales — 16 days ago.

Father David finishes the end of his drink and glances over at Mrs Hare. She sighs noisily and slouches in her chair, staring out of the café window at the grey street outside, with its grey houses, grey shops, and the grey sky above.

'Weeks, we've been here! Weeks and weeks and weeks!'

'Mrs Hare, I do believe you're bored,' says the priest, mildly. 'We've been in Wales for nine days, and in this particular town for no more than half a morning. All this fuss wouldn't have anything to do with the fact that I seem to have avoided being robbed, threatened or beaten for the last few days, would it?'

Mrs Hare sighs again. 'I've had no work to speak of since you took that walk by the docks in Swansea.'

Father David shakes his head disapprovingly. Mrs Hare frowns and adjusts her spectacles.

'I enjoy my work. What's wrong with that?'

'In your case, rather a lot, I fear,' Father David says. Mrs Hare glowers at the small priest, but says nothing.

Now Father David turns and smiles at the waitress. She smiles back and heads towards them, taking out her notepad and smoothing down her apron as she threads her way through the maze of tables to where they are sitting.

'But do cheer up, Mrs Hare! Our perseverance has paid off. I knew that if we spoke to enough people, someone was bound to tell us something, eventually. We're getting close. This is the best lead we've had.' The priest pats his jacket, where, in his breast pocket his notebook nestles. Inside, there's a page with three words written on it: GREEN DRAGON RESTAURANT.

'We have been searching in all the wrong places, but now our path is clear. Tomorrow we head for the north of Wales.' He turns to the waitress, who waits, pencil poised to take down his order, and gives her a beaming smile. 'May we trouble you for another hot chocolate with marshmallows and coloured candy sprinklings, please. Oh, and a glass of tap water.'

STRANGERS

East London — 15 days ago.

Father David is wearing dark glasses. Mrs Hare is standing beside him, her head turned to the side. Her face is a little blurred but easily recognisable. The picture shows her raising one hand to adjust her spectacles. Father David has a slight smile on his face.

Despite all the beer he'd drunk that night, the man in the brown leather jacket would never forget the oriental priest and the grey-haired lady who'd visited the White Hart two weeks ago. Skinner and Dave are still in hospital and none of the others had been back to the pub since that night. They all blame him, he knows that.

Brown Leather drops the photograph onto the table.

'Yeah. I know them,' he says.

He is called Crisp, but now his name is mud with the United Movement. Word has spread. Crisp and his boys took a beating from an old lady and a Chinese vicar. They're a laughing stock and the Movement doesn't have a sense of humour. He'll be out on his ear soon, that much is obvious, and he'll be lucky to escape another kicking, this time administered by his fascist brothers-in-arms, for bringing shame on the party.

So when the stranger called him on the phone, offering to help him get even with the cause of that shame, he was more than a little interested. He agreed to meet.

The stranger stands with his back to the window, his face in shadow.

'So this mob you're in charge of, they're like the Movement are they?' Crisp asks.

'Movement?' the stranger was still.

'Yeah, you know – the United Fascist Movement. Patriots. True Brits. You know?' Crisp squints at the stranger, trying to see his face. 'We don't like foreigners,' he adds, trying to be helpful.

'I see,' says the stranger. 'I suppose some might liken us to your . . . Movement, though our concerns are global rather than national.'

'You are English though, aren't you?' says Crisp.

The worrying thought crosses his mind that he might be dealing with one of the detested 'foreigners' the Movement taught him to hate.

'If you like.'

Crisp frowns. 'What's your name?'

'Smith,' the stranger says, after a brief pause. 'Richard Smith.' There's something in his tone. For a moment, Crisp wonders if he's being mocked.

'Now that we know each other a little better, Mr Crisp, let's talk about the work I have to offer you.' Richard Smith now exudes a reassuring air of command. His is a voice well-suited to the issuing of orders. Crisp blinks into the light streaming through the window. He nods.

'I think you'll find what I have to say most interesting,' says Richard Smith.

KILLER SWAMP

Art. Friday afternoon. Project work. No one was getting much done.

Georgette had found a book in the school library, *Horses and Ponies in Full Colour*, and she was making a sketch based on a photograph on page sixty-seven, which showed a mare suckling her foal.

Half an hour had passed. Georgette sat, pencil in hand. She had drawn one minuscule hoof and a few blades of grass.

Adda-Leigh wasn't even pretending to work. She was telling a story.

'It's true!' She looked around her, claiming all those within earshot as her audience. 'A true story. My great-granddad told it to me. He was there. In the jungle. Years ago, when he was about twenty, during the Second World War.'

With nothing else to motivate them, the class listened. Georgette saw that Sam, sitting on the far side of the room, had laid down his paintbrush and was watching Adda-Leigh, his chin in his hand, hanging on her words.

'Granddaddy was a sergeant,' Adda-Leigh said, 'and he was in this African Division. They were fighting against the Japanese army, alongside the Indians and the Chinese and the British and the Americans and loads of other countries.

'He told me how him and his mates were always trying to spook the enemy, creeping up to their lines at night, howling and moaning like they were a pack of demons from hell. And the Japs would do the same, calling and screaming and wailing like banshees in the night-time jungle. Scary stuff.

'Anyway, one particular time, the Japanese were retreating and my great-granddad and his lot were going after them, and they pushed them back into this swamp. It was like a mangrove swamp or something, with the sea all around it and just a few narrow pathways leading in. And a whole regiment of Japanese soldiers were trapped there.

'So darkness fell and great-granddaddy and a few of his men went creeping into the swamp to put the fear of God into the enemy like they always did at night.

But this time there were already screams and shouts coming from all around. And there was gunfire too. It sounded as if the Japanese were being attacked, but nothing like that had been planned.

'So great-grandaddy went forward on his own, to see what was what. And when he saw what was going on he got himself and his patrol straight out of there, double quick.

'It was crocodiles! Hundreds of them! Great big ones! They were coming up out of the lagoons and rivulets and creeks and picking off the Japanese one by one. And in the morning there wasn't more than a handful of their soldiers left alive, and most of those had gone stark raving mad. The swamp crocodiles had eaten up a whole regiment!'

The art room was still and quiet as Adda-Leigh reached the end of her story. Miss Carver, the art teacher, who had been pretending not to listen, broke the silence.

'Erm! Quiet please. No more talking now. Work!'

Georgette lowered her gaze to her drawing. A horse's hoof lying in a tangle of grass. She shivered. She remembered what old Norman at the stables had said the other evening. Something, he said, had been frightening the horses. Something out on the marsh. It came at night.

ZULU BLOOD

The blistered and itching patches of skin on Sam's arm and back made him feel diseased, infected, unattractive, disfigured and grotesque. Along with the fear that he would start sleepwalking again, and end up at the bottom of the canal with the skeletons of old shopping trolleys, being peed on by rats, the spreading rash was a constant, nagging worry.

He visited the public library on Ordnance Street and used their computer to search online for 'skin diseases'. For a terrifying thirty minutes he scanned through descriptions of Darier's disease, lupus of the skin and severe full-body atopic eczema.

He tried taking notes but the words he wrote down — psoriasis, chythyosis, hidradenitis — meant nothing to him. His hand moved unconsciously over the page, describing coils and spirals with his ballpoint. When he stood up to leave he was surprised to see the page covered in a frenziedly repeated pattern. Stylised creatures, a sprawling nest of serpents, coiled and undulated across the lined paper.

Sam left the library convinced that he was suffering, simultaneously, from each of the conditions he'd just read about. But at a deeper level he knew this was not the case. He realised that, even as he'd clicked on the search button. Some instinct had told him he wouldn't find a diagnosis that fitted his case in any conventional medical website or dictionary of dermatology. It was no comfort. He felt alone.

Though worry about his skin was never far from his thoughts, Sam still found the outside world impinging on his consciousness now and again. For instance, he couldn't help but notice Adda-Leigh. She was too charismatic to ever go unnoticed. Sam found himself looking forward to Humanities and Art because Adda-Leigh was in his class for both these subjects. He would sit and watch the way she moved her hands when she spoke, or the way the afternoon sun fell across her cheek and neck, or the light catching on the slender silver chain she wore at her throat.

It would never have occurred to him to try to get to know her better. Girls like Adda-Leigh usually had a wide circle of intimidating friends, plus a nineteen-year-old boyfriend with a car. What could she possibly want with Sam?

But now it seemed, remarkably, that she did want something from him.

'Are you not going to invite your friend in, Sam?' Llew was in the hallway. He looked past his son to where Adda-Leigh stood on the doorstep.

It was Sunday afternoon. There had been a knock on the door of the flat. Sam's first thought was – It's Adda-Leigh! The thought came out of the blue and he dismissed the notion immediately. Why would she come to see you, blister-features? he asked himself. You're not even friends. You hardly know her. But he opened the door and there she was.

'Come on in, love,' Llew called from down the hall. 'Don't mind Sam. He can be a right lummox sometimes.'

Adda-Leigh smiled. 'Thanks!' She walked past Sam and on into the flat. He turned and trailed after her.

'Come on into the lounge, love.' Llew wheeled himself in ahead of her. 'Have a seat. We're watching the film. Where are your manners, Sam? Get the girl a drink.'

Sam turned to Adda-Leigh.

'I'm okay. Honest,' she said. 'I was just round Georgette's house, she lives up the road?'

'I know,' said Sam.

'I wanted to ask you something about the Humanities homework,' she went on. 'Georgette's not in my class for Humanities but you are. So here I am.'

'What homework?' said Sam.

'Get the girl a glass of squash,' Llew said. On the television, a noisy battle scene was in full swing, with hordes of African warriors charging a thin line of British redcoats holed up in an isolated settlement.

Sam went out to the kitchen. There wasn't any squash. He let the tap run so the water would, at least, be cold, and then he filled a glass. The glass didn't look too clean. He emptied it and filled a mug. The mug was glazed dark green inside, so any tea stains didn't show up. He tried not to think about what his dad might be saying to Adda-Leigh. It was embarrassing enough when Aaron came round and Llew would insist on telling the same smutty jokes, rude and painfully unfunny. Oddly enough, Aaron didn't seem to mind. He always described Sam's dad as 'a right laugh', but Sam hated these performances of Llew's. Quite how he'd behave now that a girl like Adda-Leigh had come round to see him he could hardly imagine. But Llew wasn't drunk, at least, so Sam had to admit there was something to be grateful for.

Back in the lounge, Adda-Leigh was sitting on the

sofa. She was wearing a jumper made of a very fluffy kind of pink wool.

Llew was talking.

'Marvellous film, *Zulu*. Mind you, I'm not sure about the casting of Michael Caine. A cockney lad lording it over a regiment full of Welshmen, now that can't be right, can it?' He looked at Adda-Leigh. 'Got any Zulu blood in you, love?'

Sam nearly dropped the mug of water. Adda-Leigh, however, didn't appear put out.

'As it happens,' she said, 'I have. On my great-grand-father's side. I've got relatives from loads of different places.' She raised a hand and began counting off on her long, curved fingers. 'I'm a quarter African, a quarter French, a quarter Jamaican and a quarter Scottish.'

'No English,' Llew said, and he nodded, approvingly. 'Don't get me wrong,' he continued, 'some of the English are okay, as people, but as a nation, well . . . Quite apart from all the crimes the English kings committed against the people of Wales –'

'Hundreds of years ago,' Sam cut in.

'Apart from their many crimes, there's also the little matter of my injury.'

Sam groaned. He sat down on the sofa next to Adda-Leigh and handed her the mug of water. She looked at it, took a small sip then put it down on the floor at her feet.

'Do you know what I was doing when I got the injury that put me in this contraption?' Llew said, slapping the armrest on his wheelchair. 'I was three floors up, in a blazing warehouse. Fireman, that's what I was, see? Well, the floor gave out and down I fell, all three stories. They pulled me out of the basement with my hair all burnt off and a nasty little break in my spine. And do you know what was in that warehouse? What it was I'd lost the use of my legs to try to save? Hundreds of pounds worth of Traditional English Breakfast Tea!'

There was an awkward silence. On the television the battle still raged. The thatched roof of the settlement was now in flames and the Zulus and the British soldiers were fighting in the blazing building.

'I'll brew up a pot if anyone fancies a cup?' Llew said. 'The warehouse owners gave me a life's supply of the stuff!' He laughed. Adda-Leigh smiled uncertainly. Sam raised his eyes to the ceiling.

'Don't take any notice of him,' he said, when Llew had wheeled himself out into the kitchen to put on the kettle. 'It's awful when he's trying to be funny.'

'Has anyone ever told him that English tea comes from India?' Adda-Leigh said.

On the television the Zulus were singing a war song and the redcoats were replying with a rousing chorus of *Men of Harlech*. Sam reached over and switched off the set.

'They show that film every year, apparently, in the mess of the Royal Regiment of Wales, on the anniversary of the Zulu War.'

'Sad,' said Adda-Leigh. 'They need to get over it.'

Sam nodded. 'I'll just give Dad a hand with the tea.'

'I'm okay, honestly. I just wanted to ask you about the homework.'

But Sam got to his feet. The sleeve of his pullover had ridden up a little, exposing the red blotching of the rash, which now covered his entire arm. He pulled the sleeve down hard, stretching it over his wrist. As soon as he was through the door, he scratched his arm vigorously.

SLEEPWALKING

She didn't stay for tea.

After she'd gone, Llew grinned up at his son, and nudged him with his elbow.

'Girls! I wondered when it'd start.'

'Dad! She came round to ask about homework!'

Llew just chuckled and nudged him again.

'Don't!' Llew had knocked against Sam's arm and the contact had triggered some ferocious itching.

'No need to get up on your high horse, now, is there, loverboy?' Llew's smiling face filled Sam with a blazing fury. The uncontrollable anger that now flared inside him so often was taking over once again. He knew he was overreacting but there was nothing he could do to stop himself. It felt as if a fireball was trapped in his chest. If he opened his mouth to speak he would probably incinerate his father alive. With a muffled groan Sam turned and ran out of the flat.

'That's it, boyo,' Llew called after him, laughing. 'You might catch her up if you hurry!'

But Sam did not head up to Gunpowder Row, the direction Adda-Leigh would have taken on her way home. Instead he turned left at the end of his road and walked past the concrete bollards and onto the old towpath.

There was a man fishing by the footbridge, his bait and tackle all around him. A tiny fluorescent float bobbed in the dark water of the canal. He looked up as Sam passed by.

'I see you decided to get some clothes on this time.' His voice sounded cracked, as if he wasn't used to speaking, or as if he hadn't said anything in a long while.

Sam stared at the angler. The man wore a black woolly hat and there was several days' growth of stubble on his face.

'What?'

'You.' The angler nodded at him. 'I've seen you.'

'What do you mean?' Sam took a step back. The angler made him nervous.

'I do night fishing, don't I? I fish at night.'

'What are you on about?' Sam took another step away from the man.

'I've seen you coming over here without hardly a stitch on you, walking over the bridge, running around on the marsh. You wanna watch it. Young kid like you. There's a lot of funny people about, you know.'

'I don't come over here!' Sam broke out into a sweat, despite the chill in the air. 'I don't! Only once, anyway. You're lying!'

'You wanna watch it. You wanna see a shrink. You're not right in the head, son. You've been over the marsh every night for the past week.'

'What?'

'Every night. Over the marsh in your jim-jams. Frightening the fish. You wanna watch it.'

'Shut up! Leave me alone!'

'All right, all right, keep your rug on!'

But Sam was gone, running onto the iron foot-bridge, his footsteps clanging and booming as he pounded up the steps and across to the far side of the canal.

He ran on through the wet and yielding marsh grass, filthy water spattering his legs. A train thundered along the embankment beside him. Sam ran with it, his wild, wordless yelling drowned out by the clank and rumble of countless iron wheels. For a while he even kept pace with the great mechanical beast.

Now the concrete fence posts that surrounded the

reservoir loomed up ahead of him. A grassy bank was built up, as high as a house, all around, so from here there was no view of the water. A few sheep, belonging to some suburban farmer, were grazing on the reservoir bank. They scattered, bleating with alarm, as Sam came sprinting towards them.

He turned sharply to avoid ploughing into the fence, but he barely slowed down as he went careering down the path leading to the pedestrian tunnel beneath the railway embankment. The tunnel was low, dank and gloomy. In wet weather it always flooded. It was flooded now.

Blood was pounding in Sam's head, throbbing under his burning skin, drowning out all thought, all sense. He ran into the tunnel and ploughed into the black water that lay over the path, half a metre deep. He skidded and fell. The water rose around him, swallowed him, embraced him.

He tore off his shirt and lay down in the darkness. He let the foul water caress the devastated skin on his back and on his arm, and for a moment, he was soothed. He was calmed.

EAT IN OR TAKE AWAY

Mynnodd, North Wales – 10 days ago.

'Look!' Mrs Hare points across the field.

Father David joins her by the barbed wire fence at the side of the road.

Two men are standing by a drainage ditch beyond the field. They have dragged something out of the water. A sheep. A sheep with no head and part of one hind leg missing.

The two men stare at the small oriental priest and his tall, grey-haired female companion. Their look is distinctly hostile.

Father David and Mrs Hare exchange glances.

'A sheep. That's the third we've seen this morning.'

'No wonder that flock we saw on the hillside were

so nervous. Something's killing them. A predator. A large predator.' Mrs Hare smiles. The talk of large predators seems to make her happy, as if now, at last, she is among friends.

Father David looks at the two men in the field. They are standing still, arms at their sides, fists clenched, staring. 'I suggest we continue on our way to the village. I will feel so much better if we can avoid any unnecessary trouble.'

Mrs Hare sniffs and turns back to the road.

'Predators do tend to make farmers rather cross!'

She picks up the two suitcases and trudges off along the uneven tarmac. Father David walks briskly ahead of her.

'We may have arrived too late,' he says. 'Predatory behaviour of this sort is a bad sign. If it's what I think it is then something is very wrong.'

They come to a row of cottages. There is a pavement now, rather than an overgrown grass verge. They turn a corner and are in the main street of a large village. There are two churches, one either end of the street. There is a pub and a post office, and a handful of shops.

But the closest shop is a burnt-out ruin, its gutted interior choked with a wild growth of bramble and creeper, its rotted beams black against the sky.

Father David stops. He looks up at the sign, still

hanging from what remains of the front wall. Through the age-old soot and the grime of years the design on the cracked plastic is still just about discernible. The sinuous curves of a dragon twine around the words GREEN DRAGON – HOT CHINESE FOOD – EAT IN OR TAKE AWAY.

SOMETHING OUT THERE

Daylight faded quickly that evening and Georgette rode Dandelion back to the stables through deepening gloom. The sky was heavy with swollen rain clouds, purple-grey and blotched like severe bruising, faintly lit by the last glimmers of the dying sun.

She rode down the track that ran between the railway and the flyover, keeping Dandelion to a walking pace. The thick banks of sedge and bracken were wreathed in shadows. Georgette tried not to think about what Norman had said to her earlier that afternoon, before she set out on her ride.

'There's something out there, all right. Something weird. The horses can sense it.'

Norman was the stable manager. He took care of the deliveries of hay and feed. Occasionally, he strapped a muzzle over Lance the guard dog's vicious jaws and took him for a walk. He acted as a general caretaker to the premises. The horses themselves were looked after by their riders. Georgette didn't own Dandelion. She paid a contribution to his stabling costs, fodder, vet and blacksmith fees. She committed herself to mucking out his stall, grooming him and cleaning the tack twice a week. In return, she was allowed to ride him on Thursday evenings and every other Sunday afternoon.

'Now Dandelion there, he hasn't been too bad. But Snowy, he's been kicking all night!'

Snowy was a vicious-tempered Shetland pony. Georgette didn't think it would take much for him to be left out of sorts.

'And then there's Angus. He's completely off his feed. Won't eat a thing. And normally he's a total pig!'

This was true. Angus was a round-bellied grey, a horse well known for his partiality to oats and hay or fresh grass when he could get it. For Angus to be off his feed there would have to be something seriously wrong.

'It's out there on the marsh. Even old Lance is afraid of it. I reckon it comes at night and the animals can sense it and it's starting to get to them.'

There was an awkward silence. Georgette had a brief memory-flash of the phone conversation she'd had with her mother the night before. A silence had fallen on the line. Georgette's mother had filled it.

'Oh, you're nothing like the twins, are you, Georgie? Nothing shuts them up. They're on their mobiles morning noon and night talking to all their friends.' It was clear from her tone of voice that she thought this was something marvellous.

Georgette preferred not to speak too much, even to Adda-Leigh. Certainly she didn't usually speak to Norman at all if she could help it. She just nodded or shrugged at appropriate moments while he rambled on. She came to the stables to ride, not to talk, and besides, Norman was old, his nose was distressingly red and pockmarked and he smelt of old chip fat and pickled onions.

But now she asked him, 'What do you think it is?'

Norman looked at her through his watery, pale blue eyes.

'I don't know what it is. But if it scares Lance, then by heck it scares me too. Enjoy your ride!'

Georgette shivered at the memory and urged Dandelion into a trot for the remaining stretch of the journey back. The lights of the stables blazed up ahead, a welcome sight. She turned in her saddle and looked over her shoulder. Was that a movement back there, deep in the shadows beyond the track?

AIR AND WATER

Sam lay back in the bath. The steam from the hot water tap, which he'd left running, rose to the ceiling, swirling like tendrils of fog. The water was very hot, but he felt no discomfort.

In the bathroom cabinet, Sam had found an old bottle of bubble bath. He and Llew didn't bother with such things now. Sam remembered where this particular bottle had come from, why it hadn't been thrown away. It was a Mother's Day present. Probably the last one he had ever given her.

Amber Forest — Soothes and Invigorates, he read on the bottle. Sam poured a stream of the thick orange fluid into his bath.

The bubbles, frothing on the surface of the water, saved him from seeing his skin. The rash was on the march again. It had grown from a tiny outpost, to a fortified stronghold, to a central power with an overseas colony, and now it was embarking on the establishment of a fully-fledged global empire.

His back was a mass of puckered blisters and flaking red skin. His arm was covered from wrist to shoulder. Now there were new patches, itching and throbbing on his calves, at both ankles, at the back of his knees and behind his ears. It was taking him over.

He let his head slide down under the hot soapy bath water. A few hours ago he was lying submerged in ice-cold, stagnant marsh water in the darkness of a flooded foot tunnel. But now, this hot soapy bath he was having hardly felt any different. That didn't seem right. Was he losing the ability to distinguish between cold and hot, between clean and dirty, between normal behaviour and – well, the sort of behaviour that led one to lie down in flooded tunnels?

It was a worrying thought. To try to dispel it, he shook his head vigorously. The water churned around him. With a jolt, he realised that his face was still submerged. He wasn't breathing.

Sam broke the surface with a gasp. But there was no ache in his lungs, no sense of a desperate craving for oxygen. Could he now no longer even distinguish between air and water?

ELVIS HAS LEFT THE BUILDING

Break time, Monday morning. Sam was at school, walking slowly around the outside of the main building. It was dank and chilly, and the thick fog of the early morning was only just beginning to lift. He was alone. The other pupils were in their form rooms or in the canteen or pushing through the busy corridors, all caught in the bustle and clamour and heat of school life.

There was a tree growing up through a small square of bare earth cut into the asphalt near the teacher's car park. Some kind of fungus was attacking it, causing the bark to split and peel away. Sam remembered noticing this tree on his first day at the school, back in Year Seven. The tree's bark hadn't got any better the whole time he'd been at the school. It was diseased and the disease was permanent.

The outside door that led back to the Language classrooms was thrown open, crashing back against the wall. A figure stood on the steps, arms outstretched, as if expecting the adulation of a vast crowd. Aaron. He held a piece of toast with a bite out of it in one hand and an open packet of crisps in the other. Crumbs from both were scattered evenly down the front of his sweatshirt.

He dropped the pose and pointed at Sam.

'Sammy! What're you doing out here?' Aaron jogged down the concrete ramp and over to where Sam stood, by the diseased tree.

'What's with the turned-up shirt collars?' He gestured with his toast. 'You look like Elvis!' Aaron performed a gyration of the pelvis and essayed a parody of the Elvis Presley singing style. 'Uh-hu-hu – Oooh yeah – thangyouverymuch!'

Sam looked at him. 'Aaron. I'm not in the mood, all right?'

'Please yourself. You want a crisp?' He thrust the packet towards Sam's face. The sudden movement triggered something in Sam and he leapt back in alarm, in a violent, instinctive jolt. Aaron boggled at him. 'Jumpy!'

'Yeah. Sorry. Look, I'm not feeling that great at the moment.'

'Go to the office,' Aaron suggested. 'I'll go with you. You'll get out of PE with old Slough.'

'Is that what we've got next?' Sam felt the blistered skin on his legs begin to itch and throb beneath his school trousers. There would be no way of hiding it in PE.

He set off towards the field at the back of the school.

'Oi! Where you going now?' Aaron struggled to keep up. 'Slow down, will you? I'm spilling me crisps!'

'I'm not doing PE. I'm just not doing it.' Sam strode onto the wet grass and quickly reached the wire mesh fence at the back of the field. The fence was at least six metres high.

Aaron, breathless, jogged behind him. 'What're you doing, Sam?'

Sam turned. 'The teachers watch the front gate, don't they? So I'm going out this way.'

'Don't be stupid, you can't climb that fence. Besides, you'll get found out. They'll do the register. You've already been in trouble with the Head. Sam, this ain't like you.' Aaron still held the toast and crisps in his hands. He glanced at them with a look of irritation on his face. 'This ain't your style.'

Sam shook his head vigorously from side to side, but he said nothing. He let the straps of his backpack slip from his shoulders and the bag thudded to the ground. Then he leapt at the fence, his fingers clamping around the wire, his feet seeking toeholds in the mesh. Within a few seconds he had reached the top and swung himself over.

His body had taken charge of the action. A passenger in his own skin, he gawped down at Aaron. Then he dropped to the ground, his knees bending as he landed, easily absorbing the shock. He did not even stumble.

Aaron stared through the mesh. The crisp bag dropped from his fingers and fell, the contents scattering on the muddy ground.

'You been down the gym, or what?' Despite the attempt at humour, Aaron sounded shaken.

'No,' said Sam. 'I've been over the marsh.' He turned and started walking along the pavement and away from school.

'I ain't dragging your filthy old bag around with me if that's what you think!' Aarron yelled, his voice still a little unsteady. 'I'm leaving it here!'

Sam didn't turn. As he walked away, he heard Aaron, who must have made a supreme effort to recover his poise and sense of humour, intone with hands cupped around mouth to imitate a PA announcement, 'Ladies and gentlemen, Elvis has left the building!'

DARKER THAN THE NIGHT

Mynnodd, North Wales — 10 days ago.

Father David looks at his watch. The sun is setting, turning the mountains beyond the village to red gold.

'I wonder why she wouldn't see us this morning,' says Mrs Hare.

'I expect she wanted to prepare herself.' Father David sets off along the road through the village. 'This will not be easy for her. It is hard to talk about something that is almost impossible to believe in.'

They pass the ruins of the Green Dragon restaurant. They pass the Post Office. They pass a terrace of stone cottages. A curtain twitches in one of the windows.

'It was rather fun waiting in the pub though, didn't you think?' says Mrs Hare. 'You certainly surprised the locals. Me too, for that matter. I had no idea you spoke Welsh!'

Father David allows himself a brief smile.

'I'm not so sure about the predator, though,' Mrs Hare says. 'We may have got the wrong end of the what's-it. I was talking to one of the sheep farmers and he said he thinks it's a —' Mrs Hare breaks off. Father David has stopped and is staring ahead.

'I believe our host has come to meet us.'

Outside the last house in the village, a large, slab-sided edifice standing in isolation beyond the end of the terraced cottages, stands a large, slab-sided woman. Even at this distance she has a presence that is reminiscent of the glowering mountains dominating the horizon.

'I wonder, Mrs Hare, if you'd mind me talking to Mrs Evans alone,' says Father David. 'It has just occurred to me that she may speak more easily if she is not outnumbered.'

Mrs Hare shrugs. 'If you think it would help,' she says. The priest is in no danger. There is no work for her here. 'I quite fancy a stroll, in any case.'

The sun has set and light is quickly fading from the sky. Mrs Hare strides back down the street, hands in the pockets of her anorak. In less than a minute she is beyond the village. There are fields on either side of the road. The fields are spread with shadows.

Idly, she adjusts her spectacles with one hand. Then she freezes. Her instincts tell her she is being watched. And she senses that the eyes currently boring into her are the eyes of a hunter.

Slowly, she turns. In the middle of the road, illuminated by the lights of the village beyond, there is a large creature, darker than the night. There before her, keeping perfectly still, its powerful shoulders tensed, its green eyes fixed upon hers, is a fully-grown panther.

LOST PROPERTY

Georgette and Adda-Leigh walked along Gunpowder Row. It all seemed perfectly natural. Georgette still didn't understand why Adda-Leigh had picked her as a friend, and she was not quite at ease enough to actually ask her, but there was no doubt there was a growing sense of companionship between the two girls.

'I found it.' Adda-Leigh shook Sam's backpack. She held it in front of her, undid the catch and thrust one arm inside.

'Should you be doing that?' Georgette raised her eyebrows. Adda-Leigh just looked at her.

'Why not?' She pulled out an exercise book. 'What's this?'

'English rough book.'

Adda-Leigh read from the hand-written panel on

the front of the book. 'Sam Lim-Evans. 9S. Ms Fletcher.' She let the pages flap open. 'Aha! Doodles.' The back page was covered in drawings, scribbled in blue ballpoint.

'Where did you find his bag?'

'On the field. I heard that Aaron saying Sam had left it there. Now, what do these doodles say about his inner-self?' Adda-Leigh waved the rough book at Georgette. 'What do you think they are, snakes or something? Maybe he's a snake in the grass!'

'They look more like sea-serpents,' Georgette squinted at the page, which was covered in sinuous coils and rippling fins. 'Or dragons. Chinese dragons. He certainly likes drawing them, whatever they are. So why did he leave his bag on the field?'

'He dumped the bag, climbed over the fence and just walked off, apparently.'

Georgette frowned. 'He was bunking off school? That doesn't sound like Sam. What's up with him, lately?'

'That's what I'm going to find out. Coming?'

Georgette pulled a face. 'Do I have to?'

'You don't have to.' Adda-Leigh put the book back in the bag and drew out an ink-stained plastic pencil case. 'I just thought you might come with me, that's all.' She unzipped the pencil case, looked inside, wrinkled her nose and quickly put the case back in the bag.

'His dad's in a wheelchair. Used to be a fireman. He's from Wales.'

'Is that supposed to persuade me?'

'I'm just saying.'

'I know all that, anyway. They live near where I do, remember?'

Adda-Leigh sighed. 'Please come with me. Normally I'd go on my own but –'

'But what?'

'There's something a bit strange about all this.'

'*He's* strange, Sam is. I told you. And so's his dad.'

'What you said about seeing Sam on the marsh –' Adda-Leigh was looking at the pavement. 'It sounds a bit weird. Maybe he's ill? Maybe he needs help?'

Georgette said nothing.

'So will you come with me? To Sam's flat?'

'I can't. I'm sorry. I have to get home.'

She regretted the words as soon as they were out of her mouth. But that was that, they couldn't be unsaid now. Adda-Leigh had asked for her support and Georgette had let her down.

If she'd asked for something simple, like helping with her science homework, she would have said yes straight away. But to call at the flat in Dartmead Lane . . .

Georgette had never liked Sam's dad. He frightened her. Sometimes he came into the Ferryman's Arms and got horribly drunk. Then Georgette's father, or one of the barmen, would have to wheel him home come closing time. Georgette, lying in bed in her attic room, two floors above the bar, could plainly hear him cursing King Edward of England and singing songs in slurred Welsh.

'Sorry,' Georgette said again.

'Okay.' Adda-Leigh spoke quietly. There was a resigned tone to her voice, as if she had been expecting Georgette to let her down all along.

They turned into Dartmead Lane in silence. Adda-Leigh stopped outside Sam's flat. Georgette hurried on.

'See you later.'

'Yeah. See you in school'.

Georgette glanced back once, just as she was passing under the railway bridge. Adda-Leigh was still standing outside the flat with the backpack in her hands.

THE STING OF TEARS

There were two pints of milk in the fridge, along with some processed cheese slices, a packet of glazed ham, a tub of margarine, mostly used up, and a pot of strawberry yoghurt two days past its sell-by date.

Sam ate everything, along with half a sliced white loaf from the breadbin.

Llew didn't always keep his appointments with the physiotherapist but he had today. Sam had waited until his father left for the clinic. Llew ordered a taxi, snapped at the driver and fussed loudly while his chair was loaded into the back of the cab. When he'd gone, Sam had crept back to the flat.

He had been on the marsh since he'd left school that morning. On the marsh, in the tunnel, under the embankment, beneath the cool, dark water.

He changed out of the sodden, filthy rags that, this morning, had been his school uniform. Catching sight of himself in the bathroom mirror, he quickly looked away. The rash had spread. Apart from his face and hands, there didn't seem to be even the smallest patch of skin left that hadn't been affected by the blistering, flaking inflammation.

Wearing a clean pair of trousers, but no shirt, he walked into the living room and sat down on the sofa. He forced himself to look closely at the skin on his arm.

Tears began rolling down his cheeks, stinging him as they dropped from his jaw onto the raw skin of his chest. His head drooped forward and his shoulders shook. He let the crying take hold of him.

He would have to tell his dad now. Whatever was wrong with him, it was obviously serious. But even as the thought formed Sam knew that he wasn't going to act on it. The urge to keep his condition secret had gone beyond embarrassment or fear. Now it was a compulsion, a necessity. Tears continued to pour down his cheeks.

He heard the tentative knock at the front door and quickly stifled his sobs. After a pause, there came a more confident barrage of knocks. Another pause, longer this time. Sam sat listening, his face wet with tears. There was a final hopeless rap at the door, after

which he heard Adda-Leigh's footsteps recede down
the front path and away.

LET THE WIND TAKE THE PIECES

The flat was quiet. A clock ticked. The water hissed through the pipes in the walls. The floorboards, the beams and joists, and the wooden doors and window frames, they all creaked and sighed, almost imperceptibly, swelling and contracting in the damp weather: the slow breathing of the building.

Sam listened. He sat on the sofa with his shirt off. He didn't seem to feel the cold any more. And yet his senses hadn't dulled. Quite the reverse in fact. His nostrils twitched at the rich cocktail of smells that wafted up from the fabric covering the sofa, the foam and springs inside it, the old carpet on the floor, the worn floorboards beneath the carpet. Daylight filled the room, illuminating a galaxy of dust particles orbiting in a formless pattern, ornate but random, riding the gently shifting air that he could feel moving across his blistered skin.

And Sam was dimly aware that another sense was at work. How did I know, he wondered, that Dad was going to the clinic today? How did I know? I wasn't watching the house. I was nowhere near. I was over on the marsh. And yet I knew he had gone. It's as if I watched him leave. I can still hear him, nagging that poor cabby.

And what about Adda-Leigh? Knocking on the door of the flat. Three times, she knocked, before walking away. How did I know it was her? Perhaps it's all in my mind. I've no way of proving who it was, and even if I'm right, it could just be a lucky guess. It seems real though, as if I actually saw her there, heading off towards Gunpowder Row. Wearing her long coat with the fake fur trim around the collar. Leaving something for me, outside the front door.

Leaving something?

Sam got a long-sleeved sweatshirt from his bedroom and pulled it on. He went to the front door.

When he opened the door he was not surprised to see his schoolbag on the doorstep. It was as if he knew it would be there. But that was impossible, surely?

A note was attached, written on a piece of lined paper torn from an exercise book, fastened to the outside of the bag with a small brass safety pin. Sam picked up the bag and pulled the note off. The message was written in mauve felt-tip pen. He recognised Adda-Leigh's handwriting, sprawling and wildly ornate, with curls and flourishes adorning every character.

Dear Sam, here's your bag, boy! What you want to leave it in the middle of the field for? I had a good look through it. I like the dragon doodles in the back of your rough book. Look, I hope you're OK. I'm afraid you might be in some kind of trouble. Please get in touch with me if I can help you. Please get in touch with me even if I can't help you!

Just keep in touch, boy!

At the bottom of the page Adda-Leigh had written her mobile number and her address. She lived at 81 Union Road, up near the school. Beneath her address she had drawn what was probably intended to be a Chinese dragon. It looked like an earthworm with a beard. She had written next to it: *Can't draw!*

Sam looked at the note for a while. Then he looked at the back of his hands. What did Adda-Leigh want? To be his friend? That was how it seemed. The thought of a friendship with Adda-Leigh set a pendulum swinging in his emotions. His unformed hopes rose to a soaring, giddy excitement before plunging rapidly to a suffocating low as the reality of his situation struck home. Who would ever want his friendship now? He was turning into a freak, his skin destroyed and his senses burning into barely controllable over-drive.

A cold wind gusted down the road. It felt cool against the burning heat of the spreading rash, now throbbing and pulsing on his hands and on his cheek, on his forehead and on his neck.

He tore up the note and let the wind take the pieces.

THE FERRYMAN'S ARMS

Eleven-thirty that night. Closing time at the Ferry-man's Arms. Georgette lay in bed listening to Llew's voice, slurred and shouting, from the street below.

'And it's come to a pretty pass when your own son, your own son, look you, when your own son doesn't even bother to come home at night! It's come to a pretty pass, I can tell you!'

She heard her father, in a quieter tone, saying something in reply. She heard the thud and clatter as he manoeuvred Llew in his wheelchair down the steep kerb.

'Don't jolt me about, man!' Llew roared out. Then, his voice changing rapidly to a plaintive whine, he added, 'Now I'm going to have to throw up, see?'

Georgette rolled over and pulled the duvet up

around her ears. She made herself think about Dandelion. Dandelion, her horse, her friend who never asked for anything, who never said anything and who she'd never let down. Dandelion, in his stall at the stables, just across the canal, out there, in the night. She failed to stop herself imagining how the marsh would look with the wind whistling through the hawthorns and flattening the grass, the whole panorama under a thick blanket of darkness.

Was there really something out there in the shadows, like old Norman said? She tried to tell herself that Sam was round at Aaron's, that he'd had a row with his dad and this was his way of getting back at him. But despite the comfortable warmth of her bed, Georgette hunched her shoulders and shivered.

A MELANCHOLY SMILE

On the 10.43 train to Waterloo Station – eight days ago.

They take their seats on the train to London, the small oriental man in his black suit and priest's dog collar, and the thin, grey-haired woman with the ruddy cheeks, wearing an anorak and a pair of glasses that are constantly slipping down her pointed nose.

Mrs Hare has her arm in a sling.

'Well. That all concluded in a most satisfactory manner,' says Father David.

He sees Mrs Hare frown and adds, hastily, 'Apart, of course, from your arm, Mrs Hare. I made the classic mistake,' Father David goes on, 'of believing something to be the way we expect it to be, rather than the way it really is. I would have been willing to swear that the creature killing the sheep in that valley was our quarry. And yet, when you think of it, why would it be slaughtering sheep, like some wild predator?'

Father David smiles. 'An escaped panther! Who would have thought! Extraordinary in itself, but it pales into insignificance compared to what we're really looking for. I succeeded in winning the trust of Mrs Evans. I believe her son was married to a woman from a Luhngdonese family. We have the information we were looking for, and the panther did not cause too much interference, luckily.'

Mrs Hare sniffs. 'Luck had nothing to do with it, Father.'

Father David strokes his chin. 'My pardon. Yes, I never would have believed it was possible to kill a big cat that way. I thought he'd bite your arm off.'

'He tried. He failed.' Mrs Hare gazed out of the window at the countryside racing by.

The priest looked at her.

'You're a remarkable woman, Mrs Hare. In all the time I've known you, I've never seen a moment's remorse, never detected an ounce of regret at the fate of those you come up against in the line of duty. Until now, that is. And your adversary, in this instance, was not even a human being.'

Mrs Hare says nothing. She continues to watch the

blurred trees zipping by, the broken pasture and the distant hills. At last she speaks.

'It was injured. Its front leg. Broken, I think. Wouldn't have attacked me otherwise. It was keen to rip out my throat, of course. But in the end it stopped fighting. Seemed to know its time was up. Left me feeling a bit of a rotter, really.'

'Time to put it behind us,' Father David says. 'We return to London. We will have come full circle. Here in Britain, our search, God willing, will end where it began!'

Mrs Hare merely nods. She doesn't take her eyes off the countryside, falling away outside the carriage window as they speed eastwards. The fingers of her good hand rest lightly on her bandaged arm. Under the dressing, the wounds left by the panther's teeth ache dully. She watches the fields roll by and her thin lips twist for a moment into a melancholy smile.

WRINKLED SILVER

The night was fading. Sam watched, enrapt.

A silver light blossomed with delicious slowness, spreading across the sky, clearly visible through the puckered surface of the water.

Delicious slowness? At any other time he would have found that a contradiction in terms. But everything was different now. How he would have chaffed at the dragging of the minutes, with nothing to do except watch the sunrise. But he was changed, now. Transformed. Whether the changes were permanent or not he couldn't tell. All he knew was that his life could never be the same again. Not after this.

He waved his palms gently, with fingers spread, and felt the ripple of water over his skin, the slight shift in the flow as his body tilted ever so slightly. He hung there, in the depths of the canal. The air that he held in his lungs gave him the exact amount of buoyancy he needed to remain suspended, afloat between the surface, which now resembled a canopy of wrinkled silver, and the deep, dark, silt-covered bed of the canal below him.

With his eyes open, gazing upwards through the dark green water, he somehow had no difficulty seeing. The fragments of waterweed, wriggling gnat larvae and floating dirt motes caused him no discomfort either. The once delicate and transparent skin on the surface of his eyes seemed to have thickened and strengthened, while his vision had lost none of its clarity. In fact, he could see more clearly than ever before.

All night long he had explored the canal. Diving down to its filthy bed, he had thrust his fingers into the layers of deep black mud and decomposing leaves. He had touched the scattered bones of small fish, animals and birds, the rusting tin cans and the mould-encrusted bottles. He had drifted up to the dimpled surface and floated to the canal's weed-grown concrete sides.

He seemed able to squeeze maximum value from the slightest glimmer of light. The moon, a lighted window two floors up in a canal-side pub, the orange glow of a night fisherman's cigarette, these were all the illumination he needed to see as clearly as if it were day.

His other senses too, were working in ways he had never before experienced. Tonight, the cocktail of scents, rising from all around, entered his consciousness like a detailed map, telling him not just where everything was, but what it was comprised of, physically. Without even looking at it, he was aware of, say, a clump of grass growing on the towpath. Tangled amongst its stems there was a multitude of other things. Some he could identify, a milk bottle top, a decomposing cigarette stub, a calcified dog turd, a caterpillar, woodlice. And there were many, many more things he could not name. And yet he knew them still, from their scent alone.

Each barefoot step he took on land, and every movement he made in the water of the canal, was somehow perfect. The broken glass on the towpath would not cut him, his feet would not permit him to stumble on the rutted ground, and once immersed in the foul, polluted water he was not dragged down to his death, but welcomed in to what was now, it seemed, his natural element.

Even from under the water, he could pick out the click of a beetle's footfall as it scurried through the undergrowth on the bank. Stranger still, he could sense the hunger of a wolf spider, hidden near by, as still as death, but tensed and ready to pounce the instant the beetle came close enough.

And on top of all this, Sam found he could remain beneath the surface of the water, on just a single gulp of air, for up to three hours at a time. He was changed. He was transformed.

II

Earth, Air & Silence

The North East London Gazette

POLICE HUNT FOR MISSING YOUTH

There are fears for the safety of local teenager Sam Lim-Evans, a police spokesman said yesterday. Sam, 14, who attends Marshside Secondary School, went missing from his home in Dartmead Lane over a week ago. His father, former Fire Brigade hero Llew Lim-Evans, 43, spoke to Gazette reporters of his anguish at his son's disappearance. 'He took no money or clothes with him. I thought he'd be back, but now he's been gone so long I really don't know what to think. We've had our differences over the years, and it's not been easy since his mother died, but Sam's a good lad. I'm in a wheelchair. He wouldn't just up and leave me on my own, would he?'

Anyone who thinks they may have seen Sam, or who has any information as to his whereabouts, should contact the missing persons' office at Glass Street Police Station.

UNDER THE BRIDGE

Georgette found Adda-Leigh waiting for her before school, under the railway bridge on Dartmead Lane. She was holding a large carrier bag with something bulky inside it.

Georgette had been avoiding her. Adda-Leigh knew it, too. It had been going on since the news of Sam's disappearance became public. He hadn't been round at Aaron's. He was gone. In the corridors at school, or in class, or in the dining hall, or out on the school field, Georgette would glance up to find Adda-Leigh regarding her in silence, her melancholy brown eyes unblinking. Georgette could think of nothing useful or comforting to say, and so she told herself it was best to say nothing.

Sam's disappearance had shaken her. She had known

him since primary school. Adda-Leigh hadn't known him long, but she liked him, liked his smile, his golden skin, so his sudden worrying absence would be hard for her to take. Georgette tried not to think about Sam at all, tried not to imagine what might have happened to him. Adda-Leigh was a constant reminder, and so she avoided her.

A reporter from the local paper, a young woman with dyed red hair, had come to the pub one evening, asking about the supposed sighting of a monster in the canal. Georgette had gone up to her bedroom feeling sick. From the floor below she heard her father roaring with laughter, treating the reporter to another vodka, laughing again, loud and harsh and hollow. Georgette thought about Dandelion and the other horses in the stables by the canal, and she worried about their safety. She wasn't as convinced as her father that the monster story was a load of rubbish. She'd been out on the marsh, whereas he hadn't. Even if the creature turned out to be not quite what the local paper was suggesting, there were plenty of human monsters around to fit the bill. Georgette remembered reading reports of hideous cruelty dealt out to horses by drunken sickos and yobs. Maybe there was some psycho gang out on the marsh. And maybe Sam had run into them.

The atmosphere at school was tense. There was an edge of hysteria to the break-time chatter, mixed with a high level of either prurient speculation or affected indifference about Sam's possible fate, according to who you spoke to.

The arrival of two police officers at lunchtime triggered a wildfire rumour that Sam had been found dead, underneath the footbridge over the canal, with a black plastic bag tied around his head. Where the story with its gruesome details had come from nobody knew. It wasn't true.

Aaron had spent two days creeping around the school with a haunted expression on his face.

'Sam's been snatched. Some nut-job got hold of him. I just know it. He's dead meat.' Georgette heard Aaron muttering to a group of avid Year Sevens.

'If it happened to him, it could happen to any one of us.' Aaron swallowed, ashen-faced. 'It could happen to me!'

He was now off sick.

And Adda-Leigh had changed. The smiling, confident girl who'd arrived at Marshside and chosen her friends without any consideration as to their status within the school, had gone. She was quiet, now. Subdued. Watchful. And she was standing under the bridge waiting for Georgette, who knew she couldn't avoid her any more. Having slowed her pace for a couple of steps, she swallowed, took a deep breath and walked briskly forwards.

Adda-Leigh watched her approach. Georgette was surprised to find that something in the other girl's large brown eyes and steady gaze reminded her of Dandelion. And yes, there was something equine about her long, sculpted face. Strange she hadn't noticed it before. She didn't think she would ever mention it, however. Adda-Leigh probably wouldn't appreciate being told she had a face like a horse.

Georgette stopped in front of her. Words were difficult. Her faced burned with embarrassment and shame.

'I know you like Sam,' she said. 'I'm sorry I've been so useless. I wish I could help.'

'You can help. Come with me.' Adda-Leigh opened the carrier bag and tipped it forwards, showing Georgette the contents. Inside the bag was something heavy, waterlogged, filthy, oozing rust-brown canal water as it shifted against the polythene.

'What is that?' But Georgette realised what it was before the words had left her mouth. It was Sam's backpack.

The Marshside Free Advertiser

ANGLER SPOTS CANAL MONSTER

Could Marshside have its very own version of the Loch Ness Monster? Angler Gary Breen thinks so. He claims to have seen a mysterious creature in the canal, near Mire Street.

'I don't know what it was, but it was huge. I saw it move under the water, and a part of it broke the surface. It had horrible scaly skin.'

Breen, 30, first became aware of something nasty in the canal when his fishing float disappeared.

'I thought I'd hooked a big fish. But then, whatever it was just shot through the water and nearly dragged the rod right out of my hand. The line snapped, otherwise I would probably have lost my rod. That's when I saw this thing moving in the water.'

Publican Stuart Johns, 38, who manages the nearby Ferryman's Arms pub, was unconvinced.

'I suppose it might be nice to think there's something other than old supermarket trolleys and broken bottles down at the bottom of the canal,' Mr Johns told our reporter, 'but personally I think anyone who believes there's a monster in there must have a screw loose.'

A Water Authority spokesman, commenting on Mr Breen's description, said the mystery creature may have been a grass snake, but he added that there were plenty of carp in the canal, some as large as a metre in length.

'The thing I saw was a lot more than a metre long,' Mr Breen said. 'I've been fishing the canal for years and I've never seen anything like it. Whatever it was,' he added, 'it was no fish.'

BENEATH HER WINDOW

Sam lay at full stretch in the pool of stagnant water, down in the dark of the tunnel under the railway embankment. He was in pain.

Stretching his legs, he pushed his feet deep into the slime at the bottom of the puddle. Despite the chilling liquid mud, the flesh on the torn and ragged soles of his feet was burning.

Five hours earlier, he had walked barefoot through the streets of Marshside. It had been a dark, moonless night but Sam's improved eyesight had allowed him to see everything as clearly as if it had been midday. His feet, however, had proved less efficient. The skin on his heels had begun to burn and itch as soon as he took his first step on the paving stones of the canal towpath.

He had seen no one. No night fishermen tonight, no insomniacs out walking the empty pavements. The last pubs had closed up hours ago and he was still too early for milk rounds or clubbers heading for home. All his senses had told him he was alone with the night and the silent streets.

81 Union Road. Of course he hadn't forgotten. Adda-Leigh's address. He moved towards her home, soundlessly drifting along the pavement, despite the increasing discomfort in his feet.

He slowed when he reached Gunpowder Row. There was the sound of an engine. A car approaching. Four men in the car. Something about them. A scent? A feeling? Fear, was it? Dread? Danger? He stepped back into the shadows.

Five minutes ticked by. No car passed. The road was empty.

Provoked by the wind, a tree waved its bare branches in the beams of a streetlamp. Wild and formless shadow shapes were thrown across the ground: a shadow puppet's nightmare.

Sam waited. He could still hear the car. It was coming.

After another three minutes it drove past, the men inside it scanning the pavements, their dead-eyed stares full of meaningless aggression, aching for someone to be there, anyone, just someone for them to hurt.

They didn't see Sam. He waited until the sound of their engine and the scent of their misery and hunger had blown away, then he crossed the street.

In Union Road he didn't need to count the houses or squint at the door numbers. He could tell which house Adda-Leigh lay sleeping in, though he had never seen it before. He didn't question his senses now, or wonder about what strange instinct informed them. He just acted. There was no time for speculation. The pain in his feet was too great. He knew he had to get back to the marsh as soon as he could.

The instinct to hide away held him fast. He felt quite unable to contact his father, or any of his friends from school. Except one.

He had meant to write a note for Adda-Leigh, just as she had written one for him. The note he had torn up. Now that he was here, beneath her window, looking up towards the room where, he imagined, her dream-filled sleep might cause flickering beams of light to be cast up onto the windowpane, he found himself lost for words.

He had brought his school backpack with him, dragged it up from the depths of the canal where he had left it and carried it, dripping like a severed head, all the way to her house. There were pens and pencils in the bag. Paper too, though more than likely too sodden to stand being written on.

He had meant to write a note but he knew now that he could not. Gently, he placed the bag on her doorstep, and hoped that she would understand the message he was leaving her: don't worry about me. I'm okay.

As he limped back to the marsh it began to rain. The trail of canal water drips his backpack had left was washed from the streets as if it had never been.

PEACE

Lambeth, South London – eight days ago.

Out of Waterloo Station and into Leake Street. Turning right into Lower Marsh then left onto Westminster Bridge Road. The shuffling figure draped in a blanket follows the small oriental priest and the tall grey-haired woman. He keeps his distance.

There are plenty of people about. It is the middle of the afternoon. The enormous, slowly rotating wheel of the London Eye can be glimpsed through the gaps in the buildings.

Father David and Mrs Hare head down Kennington Road. No one looks at the man who follows the pair, keeping several hundred yards behind them on the far side of the street. The other pedestrians only see a down-and-out, a tramp of the old school. Not a young runaway, not a chancer on the make, not a heroin addict, not a victim of capitalism. This man, with his filthy blanket, his sunken eyes and his layers of clothing, topped by a tattered brown leather jacket, looks like a derelict, an old-fashioned drink-addled tramp. A man who has fallen as low as a man can go.

It is Crisp, and he has been learning the creed of his new master. At heart, this creed is hatred, a familiar lesson to Crisp. He has used it all his life. To hate others is the only way he has found to live with himself.

The message reached him that morning, at the hostel. And sure enough, here were the oriental priest and the grey-haired woman.

Richard Smith's orders are often mysterious and harsh, but Crisp understands that he must follow them without question. He has a dim sense that he has entered a new world, in which the stakes are higher than anything snooker cues or broken bottles can even touch, a world in which picking on foreigners is seen as no more significant than the vicious scuffles of an infants' playground.

It's cold on the streets but he has his hatred to keep him warm. His hatred of the two people he now watches cross Lambeth Road and enter the grounds of the Imperial War Museum.

The huge grey naval guns on display outside the museum point at the priest and his companion as they walk in through the gates. Across Lambeth Road, the tramp imagines that the guns are still in working order. In his mind's eye, he loads an enormous brass shell into the breech of the gun, checks the elevation through open sights and then fires, obliterating Father David and Mrs Hare, pulverising them, shredding them, blowing them to atoms.

He watches as they go into the Tibetan Peace Garden, to the left of the gates. They make no move towards the museum itself.

'Enjoy your peace while it lasts,' he mutters through his stained and broken teeth. He wipes his nose on his blanket and grins.

DANGER OF DEATH

Georgette and Adda-Leigh carried the plastic bag between them. In it, Sam's backpack, slippery against the polythene, slid and shifted as they walked along the pavement. Other Marshside Secondary pupils were everywhere, all heading in the opposite direction, making their way to school. Some of the younger kids stared at the two girls quizzically, but mostly they were ignored. Dressed in the uniform of dreary grey sweatshirts and crumpled black blazers, their schoolmates passed them, drifting by in groups or alone, miserable as a sky full of rain clouds blowing down Gunpowder Row towards Mill Avenue.

Georgette and Adda-Leigh continued to walk the other way, past the chipboard factory on the corner and round into Glass Street. There were no Marshside kids here. On one side of the road was a row of small factories with one or two run-down looking houses in between them. Opposite there wasn't even any pavement, just a high wire fence, and behind that, the railway embankment with its tall straggly grass, fly-tipped mattresses and slagheaps of fire-blackened house bricks and old tin cans.

Sam's backpack had appeared on Adda-Leigh's doorstep overnight, and they were taking it to the police station. Glass Street nick, as Georgette's father always called it. That was the plan, at least.

As they came in sight of the drab building with its archaic-looking blue glass lamp above the swing doors, Adda-Leigh stopped and turned to Georgette. The plastic bag swung between them.

'I never even looked inside!'

Georgette swallowed.

'Inside what?'

'Sam's backpack. I never looked inside. Not since it turned up on my doorstep all wet and nasty looking. I couldn't.'

'That's okay.' Georgette looked at Adda-Leigh, who stared back, her eyes very round. 'That's okay, the police will look at it.'

'The police? You don't think they'll keep it, do you?' Adda-Leigh took the polythene bag from Georgette and held it to her chest.

Georgette bit her lip. 'I expect they'll have to keep it for a while. They've got experts. Pathologists, or whatever. They'll be able to examine it for clues.'

Adda-Leigh shook her head. 'I don't think I can let them have it. Not if they're going to keep it.' Clutching the bag, she walked swiftly away and turned into a side street, out of sight of the police station. Georgette hurried after her.

'But it was your idea to take it to the police in the first place! It was a good idea! I really think they need to know about this!'

'I've changed my mind. I can't have them going down Sam's bag.'

'But you went down his bag yourself the other week!'

'That's different. I gave it back to him. Now he's left it with me. To look after. I can't give it to the police.'

'Wait.' Georgette tugged at the sleeve of Adda-Leigh's coat. They stopped and stood facing each other in front of a small building surrounded by spiked railings. There was a sign on the padlocked gate: LONDON ELECTRICITY – KEEP OUT – DANGER OF DEATH.

'What if it wasn't Sam that put that bag on your doorstep?'

'Who else could it have been?'

Georgette thought of the gang she had imagined

over on the marsh, she thought of the monster in the canal. She didn't say anything. Adda-Leigh turned her face away for a moment, but then she looked Georgette in the eye.

'It was Sam,' Adda-Leigh spoke quietly, firmly. 'He gave me back his bag to look after.'

'But how do you know?'

'I just do.'

Georgette looked away. 'I still think we should give it to the police.'

'No. They're not having it. And Georgette, I want you to promise not to tell anyone else about it.'

'But –'

'Just promise me, girl.'

'Adda-Leigh! We could get into trouble!' Georgette regretted the words the instant she'd spoken them. Adda-Leigh didn't say anything. She just looked at her. Her eyes, so dark and large and so like the eyes of Dandelion the horse, suddenly filled up with tears. Georgette looked at the ground.

'All right! I promise! I promise I won't tell anyone about the backpack!'

Adda-Leigh threw an arm around Georgette's shoulders and hugged her, the bag still held to her chest. Georgette found herself woodenly patting the other girl's back with the flat of her hand. The polythene bag, with the waterlogged backpack inside it, was squashed between them and pressed into Georgette's stomach. A puff of air squeezed out of the bag. Georgette smelt the harsh reek of the canal. A cold smell, heavy with decay: it was the scent of death.

THE TUNNEL WALL

By mid-morning Sam's feet had stopped hurting him. He examined them closely. There was a new suppleness in his movements he hadn't noticed before. Sitting with his back against the dank brickwork of the tunnel wall, he twisted both legs around, bent his knees and brought his upturned feet up to within a few inches of his face. He focused his eyes on the soles, first of his right foot and then his left. The flesh was puckered, crusted over and hardened, as tough as nail or bone.

The colour puzzled him. Although his vision didn't seem to be affected by the darkness under the bridge, he wasn't sure that he was identifying these particular shades and hues correctly. If he was, then the skin on his feet was now a glowing, rusty orange, and that didn't seem possible. But then neither did spending the best part of a week submerged in freezing, filthy water and living to tell the tale. It seemed he would have to adjust to a whole new way of looking at the world.

And then suddenly he knew they were coming. The man and the dog, heading for the tunnel. He was aware of their approach long before he could hear them, and he could hear them long before he could see them. But it wasn't just the man, wheezing slightly, stumbling over the waterlogged ground, his Wellington boots chafing against a blister on his big toe, and the dog, stalking from one scent-rich clump of grass to the next with his lip curled back in a permanent snarl. Sam was also aware of other creatures on the marsh.

The beating heart of the reed bunting, clinging to a swaying bulrush, giving throat to its warning song before taking to the wing; the kestrel, hanging overhead, affecting indifference at the presence of the man in its hunting ground below; the rat, lying low in the undergrowth, wary of the man, but more wary of the dog. All these sensations reached Sam in his dark lair. And he felt just as alarmed as any creature on the marsh when he realised the man wasn't going to be deterred by the waterlogged tunnel, that he really was going to walk through it.

Sam threw himself down into the deep puddle on

the tunnel floor, but deep as it was, there wasn't enough water to hide him completely from sight. He dragged himself out again and flung his back against the wall, breathing hard.

The water slopped and churned for a while before calming to a few muddy eddies. But Sam quickly realised he had misjudged the man's approach. There was no time to escape out through the other side of the tunnel and hide in the tall grass beside the filter beds. The man's bulky silhouette was already darkening the entrance.

Sam didn't question his need to hide from the man. As with his nocturnal visit to Adda-Leigh's house, he now acted on a feeling alone. His every sense was telling him to avoid an encounter with this person.

He held his breath. He froze. He watched the man blinking in the tunnel entrance, heard his laboured breathing and the suddenly nervous heartbeat. Sam willed himself to become invisible, to appear as no more noticeable than an uneven section of tunnel wall.

The man waded into the still shifting water that filled the tunnel floor.

'Rats,' he muttered, under his breath. Then he turned back to the tunnel entrance and bellowed, 'Lance! Come on!'

He splashed through the tunnel, the water slopping

up into his boots, passed Sam without so much as glancing in his direction, and disappeared out the other side.

Sam allowed himself to let out a stream of breath through one nostril. Then Lance the guard dog came into the tunnel.

Sam watched the hackles rise on the big Alsatian's back. He saw the dog's eyes glowing orange with reflected light as it stopped and stared at him. He looked at the dog and silently begged it to be calm, to be gentle. Instantly, the dog gave an anguished howl, turned tail and bolted from the tunnel, back the way it had come.

Sam listened to the man calling the dog over and over for the next hour and watched him wade back through the tunnel again to continue calling on the other side of the marsh. The man gave up at last, his voice hoarse, and clumped off in the direction of the stables under the flyover. Only then did Sam let himself take another breath.

A SECRET IS KEPT

Seven years earlier . . .

Suzi Lim-Evans lay in her hospital bed and looked at the framed photograph her husband had left her. A picture of Sam. Her son. Her little golden boy. His school photograph. Looking out at the camera from beneath a wildly crooked fringe, not one of her better attempts at home hair dressing it had to be said, with a reluctant smile on his face.

Llew hadn't left her a photograph of himself. He wouldn't allow anyone to take his picture since he had the accident. The accident had forced him out of the Fire Brigade and into his hated wheelchair. He'd burnt all pictures from before that date. All but one, which she'd managed to hide away from him. She

kept it in an old biscuit tin on top of the kitchen cupboard. Llew aged twenty-one, smiling and gorgeous
in his uniform.

With a shock of sorrow, it struck Suzi that she
would never get the chance to look at that photograph
again. It was at home and she was here and here was
where she would stay until the day the other patients
on her ward looked up to see an empty bed. The
porters would come and wheel her away to the
morgue. That time was coming soon, she was suddenly
sure of it.

She was waiting for the priest, Father O'Connell.
He was later than usual tonight.

Suzi tossed her head in anxiety. What if something
happened to her before she had a chance to speak to
the priest? He was a rather silly man, it was true.
Young, inexperienced, a ditherer, but she knew she
could trust him. She had a secret that had to be con-
fided. A secret that she had kept all her life. Now her
life was ebbing away and the wretched man was
going to be too late! She had been careless, hadn't
wanted to believe the worst could happen. But now
she was suddenly convinced she had made a terrible
mistake.

There were no doctors about this evening. It was a
Sunday, when there was always fewer medical staff
around, and a series of emergencies were taking up the

time of those who were in today. Suzi sat up and swung her legs over the side of the bed.

Vera, the old woman in the bed opposite, looked over at her.

'Here, I wouldn't get up if I was you, luvvie. Didn't the doctors say complete bed rest for you? And you do look very poorly, dear, if you don't mind my saying so.'

Suzi grimaced. She felt a warning pain shoot through her chest.

But here was the young priest now. He wasn't too late after all. She waved to him and then beckoned. He stood still, frowned and raised his eyebrows quizzically. Finally he made his way across the ward to her bedside. All the while, the pain in Suzi's chest was building.

'Pen and paper, Father. I have to tell you something. You must write it down and give it to my son. Not my husband, he won't understand. But my son must know. He must know about the blood.'

'Now, now, Mrs Lim-Evans,' Father O'Connell said, speaking slowly and clearly, the way he spoke to the elderly, even though Suzi, despite her advanced heart condition, was actually only thirty-five years old. 'Don't fret, now.'

But the look in the eyes of this small and delicate-boned Chinese-looking woman made the priest change his tone.

'I'm sorry. I'll fetch a pen and some paper, right enough. I shan't be a moment.'

Suzi wanted to scream at him to come back as he turned away. She suddenly knew she'd no time left at all, that the priest would have to memorise her message instead, she would have to tell him everything, right now.

But the pain she was in had suddenly exploded into agony. It was as if her chest were being crushed in a vice. She couldn't speak, couldn't utter a sound. The pain was spreading down along her arms and up through her throat and into her jaw. She fell back onto the bed.

'Are you all right, luvvie?' she heard Vera say. The old woman's words floated out over a haze of excruciating pain.

'Here, is she all right? Do you think she's all right?'

Suzi tried to take a breath but it was as if her throat had been closed off.

'Should we call a nurse? I think we'd better call a nurse. Nurse! Nurse!'

Vera's voice faded into nothingness.

ANOTHER TIME,
ANOTHER HOSPITAL

Central London — six days ago.

'I looked for a pen. There was no one at the nurses' station so I took one from the desk. I'd found an old bus ticket in my jacket pocket. I was going to jot down her words on the back of it, hoping that whatever it was she wanted to say was not too long, you understand! But when I returned to the ward I saw there was some kind of commotion going on.'

Father O'Connell stops talking. He dabs at his sweat-drenched forehead with a sodden handkerchief. His hands shake convulsively as he tries to return the handkerchief to his dressing-gown pocket. He drops it on the floor.

Father David discreetly picks up the handkerchief

and hands it back to his fellow priest. They are in the visitors' room at the Royal Imperial Hospital for Tropical Diseases. Old Mrs Evans had given him the name, but it had taken four days to track Father O'Connell down.

'I'm sorry, Father David. I shall be okay in a moment. I have some rare strain of malaria and they're having a lot of trouble flushing it out of me.'

Mrs Hare stands by the door, the zip on her anorak done up to the neck, her arms wrapped around her for warmth. All the windows in the visitors' room are wide open, despite the chill of the day and the noisy grind and rumble of the traffic from the busy London streets below.

Father David sits with the shivering priest and waits patiently while he composes himself.

Father O'Connell gives a weak cough and fingers the handkerchief in his lap.

'Well, of course, when I got back to the ward, there was poor Mrs Lim-Evans with a nurse either side of her and a third bringing in the crash trolley and another one pulling the curtain closed around her bed. I stood there like a statue, pen and paper in my hand. They told me she fell unconscious and never opened her eyes again. I performed the last rites but I don't know if she even knew I was there.'

'You did what you could.'

'Oh, I wasn't any help to her! Standing there, frozen, with the pen and paper useless in my hand. It's strange, I'd seen sorrow and suffering on a far grander scale before, but it had never really touched me, not in the way the death of poor Mrs Lim-Evans did. It was then that I decided to go and work abroad, to the Far East, where I eventually fell victim to one mosquito bite too many. They shipped me back again, and so you find me here!'

'She never told you her secret?'

'No. She'd referred to it once or twice some days earlier, saying she had some kind of family secret that she didn't know whether to pass on or not. I got the feeling it was something she wasn't entirely sure if she could believe in or not. But there's no doubt in my mind, when her time came she was terribly anxious to pass the message on to her son. And I couldn't help her. I failed. It still bothers me, Father, even now.'

Father David rests his hand on the other priest's arm for a moment.

'Do not worry. I believe that with God's help, Mrs Lim-Evans' message will soon be delivered at last.'

At this, Father O'Connell puckers his brows in a puzzled frown. He opens his mouth to ask a question but then a fresh bout of shivering grips him. Father David turns to Mrs Hare.

'Will you fetch a nurse, please? I believe it is time our friend returned to the ward.'

Mrs Hare nods. She glances out of the open window as she turns to leave the room. A fire engine, its siren wailing, is weaving through the lines of traffic on the road below.

Unseen by Mrs Hare, a hunched figure stands in the doorway of a closed-down newsagent's opposite the hospital. The flashing blue light of the fire engine illuminates his face momentarily as it passes by. It is Crisp. His eyes are fixed firmly on the entrance to the Royal Imperial Hospital for Tropical Diseases.

CLOSE TO DISINTEGRATION

It was mid-morning. Outside the corner shop at the end of Furnace Road a woman was trying to push a double buggy in through the door. Far closer, down at the kerbside, a ragged-looking pigeon pecked at the squashed remains of a kebab in pitta bread. An old man with milky blue eyes, wearing an overcoat, a yellow scarf and a trilby hat, inched his way, half a shuffling footstep at a time, along the pavement. A marmalade-orange cat yawned on the windowsill of a house with a blue front door.

Workers were all at work. Schoolkids were all in school. A kind of dreary peace, in which stifling boredom walked hand-in-hand with utter contentment, lay over everything and everyone.

Everyone, that is, except Georgette and Adda-

Leigh. They were out of place and out of time. They had to get away.

'Down here! Quick!'

They ducked into an unmade driveway between two houses. Rutted tracks led down to two old garages, with walls made from sheets of grey asbestos.

Adda-Leigh squatted on the concrete slope in front of the green-painted metal doors. She tipped the plastic bag upside down and shook it. Sam's back-pack fell out and landed with a soggy thud.

Georgette stood and watched as Adda-Leigh lifted the backpack in her long-fingered hands, turned it this way and that, then tugged at the zip to open it up. She let the contents slide out and spill across the concrete slope. There was the same collection of pens, broken pencils and school exercise books that Adda-Leigh had looked through before leaving the bag outside Sam's flat, except now the books were all soaked in filthy water and close to disintegration. The rough book with the Chinese dragons in the back had reverted to pulp. There was no sign of the note Adda-Leigh had left.

'What's that?' Georgette leaned down and pointed. Something dark lay amongst the pale wads of paper mulch. Adda-Leigh lifted it between finger and thumb and held it up.

It was a strand of waterweed, its fronds still drip-ping with moisture.

'Let me look.' Georgette held out her hand. She took the piece of plant, holding it by its slippery stem.

'I recognise it.'

Adda-Leigh squinted up at her.

'Recognise it? What are you talking about, girl? It's a manky old bit of plant! You can't have seen it round the shops, or noticed it hanging about suspiciously by the school gates, or something!'

'No, I mean I've seen plants like this before. They grow underwater. I've seen tons of the stuff.'

'Where? Where have you seen it?'

Georgette took a deep breath.

'In the canal.'

A THOUSAND DEATHS

Night fell. Sam emerged from his tunnel lair. He tottered slightly. It was as if he had woken after many hours of sleep. Now that he thought about it, however, he couldn't remember the last time he actually had slept.

He blinked, and a memory surfaced from years ago. He had risen early one morning. Walking out of his bedroom, padding through the flat, his bare feet moving from dry carpet to cold lino to floorboards and onto the deep-pile rug in the lounge where he had stopped.

He looked up and there was his mother, lying on the couch in her silk dressing gown. The skin of her face looked as pale and cold as ivory, framed by her blue-black hair. Llew was next to her, in his wheelchair, still and silent, with one suntanned arm outstretched, holding her hand in his. She looked up, saw Sam, and smiled a slow, tired smile.

The memory was heavy with sadness and mystery. Whether there was any connection between that morning long ago and the discovery of the heart condition that eventually ended his mother's life, he did not know. But for Sam, that moment, when she looked up and smiled her slow smile, had become fixed in his memory as the beginning of her last farewell.

Now, standing out in the chill of the night, he blinked and shook his head to clear his thoughts. The marsh lay all around, hushed and still beneath a dark purple sky that was dusted with more stars than he had ever seen. Although the murky lights of the city spilled across the sky as usual, tonight their glare did nothing to obscure Sam's view of the firmament. He caught his breath, it was so beautiful.

But this moment of peace was short-lived. He became aware of a strange sensation. It was a little like noticing a mixture of different smells borne on a gust of wind, or feeling some minute insect crawling across the skin, or hearing a distant voice; so quiet it was almost indistinguishable from silence.

Uneasy, he looked around but saw nothing to alarm him. He was aware of no threat close at hand. In fact, he was convinced there were no people on the marsh at all. He did, however, notice the ripples of movement that ran through the nocturnal landscape. The water lapped, the undergrowth shivered, grass blades trembled. It was the true inhabitants of the marsh, the foxes, the owls, the rats, the mice, the insects, spiders, snails, slugs, earthworms and centipedes, all going about their ordinary lives.

And their ordinary deaths. It was these deaths that Sam could feel.

The feeling built in intensity, rose in volume, swelled and filled his mind with a thousand silent screams, a thousand death throes, a thousand final moments of pain and dismay.

With a horrified moan, Sam fell to his knees, his hands clutched to his ears. But the sensation was inside his head. He couldn't block it. Letting out a cry that burned and tore at his throat, he slumped forward into a ragged patch of hawthorn and lay there in the undergrowth, his knees drawn up to his chest. Hot tears spurted from his eyes and burned where they trickled over the sore and scaly skin of his face and neck. His chest heaved with silent sobbing while all around him the undergrowth rustled and shivered with small but violent movement.

THE NYMPH

Georgette came back into the living room where she'd spread her homework books out on the coffee table.

'Dad!'

She couldn't keep the surprise out of her voice. It was past eight o'clock and he was always downstairs working behind the bar at this time of night.

'Hello, Georgie.' There was an awkward silence. 'Doing your homework?'

'Yes, Dad.'

Georgette took her place, kneeling beside the coffee table. She looked down at her books. Maths. She waited for her father to go.

But he didn't. After a moment he cleared his throat.

'Erm . . . the school telephoned earlier on. Said they marked you down as an unauthorised absence today.'

Georgette nodded. She kept her eyes on her books.

'That's not like you, Georgie.' Her father sounded embarrassed. Puzzled too.

'Playing truant? That's not like you at all.'

Georgette shook her head. She felt the blood rushing to her face. She and Adda-Leigh had been caught climbing in over the school wall, halfway through third lesson, hoping to slip back into their lessons without being noticed.

'What would your mum say, eh?'

Georgette thought her mother might actually be thrilled. Georgette out with a friend, doing something daring! She opened her mouth to speak but thought better of it. Despite the way she felt, she didn't want him to hear her criticising Mum.

Her father looked at her. 'You're not going to do it again, are you?'

'No, Dad.'

'Good girl.'

Georgette glanced up at her father. She could tell he was looking for a way to end the conversation. She saw his eye fall on the jam jar she'd filled with canal water on the way home.

She'd brought back the piece of waterweed they'd found in Sam's backpack. She'd kept it in the hope that Adda-Leigh would change her mind and go to the police after all. The waterweed could be evidence. She didn't want it to dry out, so it was in the jam jar, floating in the slightly cloudy canal water.

Her father picked up the jar and peered at the contents.

'What's this? Science project? Very interesting, those creatures.'

'Creatures?'

'Don't tell me you don't know what's in there. Look!'

He thrust the jar at her. She looked. There, trying to hide amongst the waterweed fronds, she saw a pale grey, six-legged being. It had bulging eyes and an evil-ly jutting lower jaw.

'What is it?' Georgette wrinkled her nose with distaste. 'A fish? A shrimp?'

'No, it's a dragonfly! Or it will be when it grows up. They call them nymphs. They're like the dragonfly version of a tadpole, only these things sometimes stay in the water for a couple of years before they grow up properly.'

Georgette looked at her father.

'Now don't look at me like that!' he said. 'I do know some things about nature. I'm not a complete ignoramus, just because I run a pub. I love animals, me. Talking of which, I'd better get downstairs. That new barmaid is a right dozy cow!'

TO WATCH AND TO WAIT

East London — three days ago.

Mrs Hare pauses in the act of pulling the curtains closed. She glances over at Father David, lying on one of the twin beds with his shoes off.

'Why is it, Father, that you always get to choose which bed you sleep in?'

Father David raises his head.

'Would you prefer this bed, Mrs Hare?'

'No. It's all right.'

'You're quite welcome to it. One bed is very like another in these places.'

'You're right, Father. Stay where you are. I'll have the bed by the window.'

Father David lies back on his pillow. Mrs Hare turns

back to the garish floral-patterned curtains. With a swift movement of both hands she draws them together, blocking out the night.

Outside, in the darkness, Crisp has been watching the window of the run-down Guest House. He stays where he is, hidden by the shadow of the low-rise flats opposite. For the time being he is content just to watch. To watch and to wait.

THE FACE IN THE MIST

Sam twisted and flailed on the ground. He clasped his hands to his face. He moaned and shook his head repeatedly from side to side.

He couldn't block out the pulsing, burning, screaming, ever-turning wheel of life and death on the marsh. He felt as if his mind would soon buckle and cave in under the weight of this horror, and that he would be lost to pain and despair for ever.

Time passed, second by second, drip by drip, each slowly passing minute bringing new horrors.

Eventually, however, a numbness began to form around his fear. Deep down he realised that at some unconscious level he could understand how to live with what he was now experiencing. He groped towards that understanding, like someone trapped in a smoke-filled building, staggering blindly towards the location of the fire exit.

But he knew he couldn't reach it without help. What he needed, he thought, was to fix on one image, something he could use to ward off the terror of the night, something real and precious. He had to think of something. Or someone.

Through the blood-coloured mist swirling behind his tightly closed eyes a picture was slowly forming. It was the image of a face. The face of Adda-Leigh.

Sam focused on the image and felt his fear and misery begin to fall away. The creatures of the marsh were still hunting and killing and hiding and fleeing, but gradually he began to understand them. As his pounding heartbeat slowed its pace, the terrifying mental pictures that had been haunting him turned slowly into musing thoughts.

This was their world, the world of the marsh-dwellers. They were part of it, and they accepted it, for all its brutality, because its terrors and sorrows were balanced by its ferocious joys. Sam no longer felt overcome by the mindless agony all around him. Instead, as he thought of the marsh creatures, he felt the touch of an inexpressible pleasure at their being, the breath in their nostrils, the beating of their hearts and the wild, pulsating wonder of their existence.

As dawn broke over the marsh, Sam looked around

him with the dazed relief of one who has been in the grip of the most appalling torment but has escaped, somehow, unscathed.

And now, in everything he looked at, the gently waving grass blades, the rippling surface of a marshy pool, the sky itself, endless and beautiful, laced with ribbons of delicate yellow cloud, in all these things he saw the face of Adda-Leigh.

ROUND AND ROUND

Georgette was riding Dandelion around the indoor arena while over her head the motorway thundered and roared.

But she was not happy. Too many thoughts were crowding in on her and she had no way of chasing them out. The riding wasn't enough any more. She circled the arena, and her worries, too, went round and round, inside her head.

Adda-Leigh had phoned her earlier that Saturday morning.

'Hello. It's me. I had a dream last night.' She'd sounded out of breath; her voice was tight, strained. 'I dreamed I was floating over the marshes like a big old balloon or something. I was sure there was someone else there, down on the ground, but I couldn't see anyone. Just filthy old grass and puddles of mud. But I was sure someone was there.'

There was a pause before she went on. 'Georgette. What if it means something? My dream. What if Sam's laying out there, dead, killed, buried somewhere on the marsh? I'm scared, girl.'

Georgette was scared too, but she couldn't see the point of telling that to Adda-Leigh.

'Look, don't worry. Everything will turn out okay, somehow.' It was all she could think of to say. But her words had sounded hollow and meaningless the moment she'd uttered them. She had left home to go for her morning ride feeling troubled.

The atmosphere at the stables was no help. Norman the caretaker was sitting in his damp little office, huddled over the electric bar heater, when Georgette arrived earlier that morning. She proffered the envelope with her subscription money inside it, the money that went towards Dandelion's feed and stabling costs, but he barely even glanced up.

'Not seen Lance, have you?' he said. His voice was flat and lifeless.

'Isn't he tied up outside?' Georgette instinctively glanced about her, as if to make sure the guard dog wasn't lurking in the corner next to the filing cabinet.

'He ran off. Yesterday, on the marsh. I've not seen him since.'

Georgette's first reaction to this news was a secret rush of relief. Lance was a vicious animal and his brooding presence, chained up out in the yard, had been unsettling at the best of times. But Norman went on.

'You read the local paper? There's something nasty out there. On the marsh. There's been sightings. I reckon it got him.'

Norman climbed laboriously to his feet and moved over to the small office window.

'I don't care much about Lance. He was a nasty piece of work. But we could do with a guard dog here at the moment.'

He gazed out through unfocused eyes.

'Someone ought to stay at the stables overnight. The horses need somebody to keep an eye on them. But there's no way I'm doing it now that Lance has gone. No way at all.'

Georgette had put her money down on the desk and left Norman standing at the window.

Now she rode around and around the arena while outside the rain lashed down and above her head the traffic rushed heedlessly by. By now, her thoughts had lost all consistency. A meld of anxiety over the missing Sam, an imagined gang of psychos, withheld evidence, the police, monsters on the marsh, lost guard dogs and vulnerable horses churned around her mind in a formless mass of worry.

But she leant forward and patted Dandelion's neck, in truth trying to reassure herself rather than the horse, which was trudging passively around the paddock.

'I won't let anything hurt you, Dandelion,' she whispered. Then she gritted her teeth and fervently hoped she could live up to her words.

SEARCHING . . .

The lashing rain formed a curtain across the entrance to the tunnel under the embankment. Inside, Sam sat with his back to the wall, still and silent in the gloom.

An idea had taken hold of him. It was proving just as persistent as the blind instinct that had driven him to hide out on the marsh. He wanted to phone Adda-Leigh.

He had not forgotten the mobile number written on the note she'd left him, any more than he had forgotten her address. The sequence of digits had imprinted itself permanently onto his mind's eye. Now, sitting in the dark, he found himself dwelling on the numbers, wordlessly sounding out the pattern inside his head, tasting the weight, the texture, the value of the sequence and trying to project each numeral as a distinct pulse of cerebral energy.

Thoughts that had begun as a piece of dreamy meditation were quickly becoming something more solid. He felt his fingers twitch and flex, as if punching in the numbers onto a keypad, one by one. But there was no keypad. There wasn't even a phone.

He formed the sequence and then kept it intact, holding it together in its translated, electronic form, a pulse, cradled within a suspended thought wave. Meanwhile, he also reached out into the ether, seeking the correct frequencies and the corresponding signal he needed to establish contact.

These two simultaneous tasks defeated him. He felt the carefully constructed number sequence wobble and then collapse and scatter like a tower of building blocks. But he had a taste for it, now. He remained still and silent in the gloom of the tunnel. He gathered his thoughts, and started the process again.

L

Marshside, north-east London — yesterday.

Father David lifts the telephone receiver. He opens the phone book and turns to the residential numbers, finds the Ls. The thin pages rustle as he leafs through them. Lester, Levy, Lewis, Lilly. He runs his finger down the page. Lim. Lim-Evans. Just the one entry:

LIM-EVANS L.
3b Dartmead Lane . . . . (020) 6137 9692

The priest turns and looks at Mrs Hare, standing silently behind him in the hallway of their Bed-and-Breakfast. They exchange looks. He pushes a coin into the slot on the old payphone and carefully presses in the numbers, checking each one on the scratched display screen before continuing.

'It's ringing,' he says.

They continue to stare at each other in silence. Then Father David suddenly starts and takes a firmer grip on the receiver. At the other end of the line, someone has picked up the phone.

THE ICON

Georgette was not particularly interested in her mobile. She was always forgetting to top up the credit, was slow at texting and found ring tones boring. She left her phone at home when she went riding.

When she returned to the Ferryman's Arms she found that Adda-Leigh had left her a voice-mail message asking to meet her under the railway bridge at one o'clock. She looked at her watch. It was ten to.

Adda-Leigh was waiting for her, just as she had been the other morning. But this time she was wearing jeans and a denim jacket, not school uniform. She started talking before Georgette had even reached her.

'You know Aaron? Fat Aaron. He's a friend of Sam's?'

'Yeah,' Georgette replied, slowly. There was a wariness to her tone that Adda-Leigh ignored.

'You know where he lives?'

'Yeah. On Mire Street. The house on the corner, up by the main road. Why?'

Adda-Leigh set off immediately, walking along the pavement beneath the bridge.

'I thought he might help us look. He's supposed to be Sam's friend, isn't he?'

'Help us look? What do you mean?' Georgette had to jog to catch up with the other girl, who was walking at a furious pace. 'Look for who?' But she knew what the answer would be.

Adda-Leigh didn't bother to reply. Instead she turned and stopped suddenly, and stood facing Georgette in the middle of the pavement. She almost slammed straight into her.

'He rang me, George. He rang my mobile. It was him. I'm sure of it.'

'Sam? Sam rang you?'

Adda-Leigh nodded. There was a silence. The two girls stared at one another.

'What did he say?' said Georgette, after a moment.

'He didn't say anything. We were cut off.'

'But you're sure it was him? You know his number?'

Adda-Leigh looked away.

'It was weird,' she said. 'There wasn't a number. My mobile rang but nothing came up on the screen. No name, no number. Just this funny little icon. I've never seen anything like it.'

'Why do you think it was Sam?'

'It was him. I just know it. He might be trapped somewhere, held prisoner, I don't know. Maybe he's just got hold of a mobile and my number was the only one he could remember.'

'Not his home number? Not 999?'

'Look, I don't know, do I?' Adda-Leigh was angry, exasperated. 'I just know it was him, don't ask me how.'

'Did you look in received calls?'

'No good. There was nothing there. Just that weird icon. Then that vanished, too.' Adda-Leigh was on the move again, turning into Mire Street with Georgette hurrying at her heels.

'What kind of icon?'

Adda-Leigh pounded over the pavement, staring ahead of her.

'It looked like a dragon,' she said.

THE CALL

Sam's nerve had gone the moment he heard her voice when she answered the phone.

'Hello?' One word. But that one word carried with it the sound of her voice, the whisper of her breath, the movement of her face, her throat, her hand gripping the phone, and all these things had summoned up her very essence. Overcome by anxiety, Sam had allowed his painstakingly constructed mental signal link to break down and the call was disconnected.

He tried to start again, but he found he couldn't do it any more. The reality of Adda-Leigh's voice sounding inside his head was too impossibly intimate for him to bear. He knew in his heart of hearts that no good would come of it. So much simpler to obey his first instincts and remain hidden, here on the marsh, seeing no one, speaking to no one.

But what of the impulse to contact her? Wasn't that also instinctive? Filled with confusion, Sam shook his head vigorously. He felt a pressing need to be moving. Another ill-defined instinct was exerting its pull. With his mind whirling, he let his body take control. Without a sound, he rose to his feet and moved to the entrance of the water-filled tunnel, barely ruffling the surface of the pool as he passed.

Out on the marsh some people were walking their dogs. There were a few joggers, one or two anglers on the canal, a man on a bench drinking a can of extra-strength lager, youth footballers, and the raucously bellowing fathers and mothers who watched them on the playing fields the far side of the motorway.

But despite the presence of all these people, Sam felt confident he wouldn't be spotted. He crossed the stretch of marsh grass in fits and starts, blending in to his surroundings, hugging the ground where necessary, freezing when he felt any eyes turn his way. In less than three minutes he had scaled the barbed-wire-topped concrete fence and slipped into the still and icy waters of the reservoir without so much as a splash.

He had heard the call of deep water, and he had answered that call. With his arms stretched out in front of him and his toes pointing back towards the surface he let gravity direct him downwards. He sank into the inky darkness like a stone.

A PARTING OF WAYS

Georgette followed Adda-Leigh up Mire Street.

'Addie, listen. I don't think we should look for Sam any more. Not you, not me, not Aaron. I think you have to tell the police where you think he is and let them look for him themselves.'

Adda-Leigh stopped and spun round to face Georgette.

'And what exactly should I tell them? That I had a dream that told me where to find Sam?'

'This is serious, Addie. Sam really has gone missing. We won't be able to sort this out for ourselves.'

'Is that what you think I'm doing? Trying to solve a mystery like the kids in Scooby-Doo, or something?'

'No, but –'

'But what? You just haven't got the guts to help me!

You of all people!' Adda-Leigh clenched her fists, her eyes tightly closed. She took a deep breath. 'When I first came to Marshside I thought, right, I'm not going to make the same mistake I've made at other schools. I'm going to be friends with whoever I want, nothing to do with how fashionable they are, or whether they're one of the so-called cool kids, or any of that rubbish. I saw you and I thought, here's a girl I can trust, and I saw Sam and I said, here's a boy I can love.' Tears were in her eyes. 'Now he's gone and I need you to help me find him. Don't tell me I was wrong about you?'

'Adda-Leigh, stop. Let's just calm down and think this through.'

'No. Calmness is not what we need at the moment. We have to do something, now. If you won't help me, I'll make do with Aaron. You don't even like Sam, do you? You probably don't even care if he never gets found!'

'That's not true!'

'I'm going to get Aaron, then we're going to the marsh. Are you coming or not?'

Adda-Leigh, nostrils flaring, looked Georgette in the eye. Georgette held her gaze for a moment, but made no reply. She looked down. Adda-Leigh gave a snort of contempt, turned and walked away, leaving Georgette standing alone on the pavement.

MARSH BOUND

Bus Number M23, on Gunpowder Row — that evening.

Mrs Hare and Father David sit in the front seats on the top deck of the bus. The street lamps are alight, shop windows glow and televisions flicker in the front rooms of the houses as they pass by.

'Are you sure we should be going there now? It's dark! How are we going to find him in the dark?'

'We must begin the search, Mrs Hare. You heard what the boy's father had to say before he hung up. All the signs are there. Sam would have headed for the nearest stretch of water.'

'Well, we could have had some dinner first.'

The bus driver's gruff shout from the lower deck interrupts them.

'Mire Street! This stop for the marshes!'

Father David beams. 'How helpful of the driver to let us know!'

He makes his way down the stairs and Mrs Hare follows him, glancing anxiously about her. She straightens her glasses and frowns.

'I don't like this, Father,' she says, as they step out onto the pavement. 'Ever since we got back from Wales, I've had a bad feeling. It's the same feeling I had when that panther was creeping up behind me. Something's not right. I don't know if I can do my job properly any more. Not sure I've got any fight left in me. I wish I hadn't had to kill it. The panther, I mean. I just don't feel right any more.'

But Father David merely turns to her and smiles. Then he steps out into the road. With a yelp of alarm, Mrs Hare drags him back onto the pavement as an eight-wheeled truck thunders by, missing him by a few centimetres.

'You see, Mrs Hare?' the small priest is still smiling. 'We have nothing to worry about. You will always keep me safe.'

There is a gap in the traffic and Father David walks across the road at a leisurely pace.

'There's Mire Street, just opposite. Come, Mrs Hare, the marsh awaits us!'

'Okay,' Mrs Hare mutters under her breath. 'I'll

watch your back, Father. But who'll be watching mine?'

By this time the bus they alighted from has reached its next stop, which is quite close, only a hundred metres or so along the road. A man who had been slumped in the corner seat at the back of the lower deck now shuffles along the aisle and climbs out onto the pavement. He stands at the bus stop and watches as Mrs Hare and Father David cross the road and head down Mire Street.

MARSH HUNTED

Sam looked up through the filter of the reservoir's surface as daylight bleached from the sky and night came to the marshland. The numbing cold of the deep water calmed his nerves as once it had soothed his burning skin. Whatever had caused that aspect of his condition no longer seemed to be troubling him, and now his nameless fears were fading away, too.

He gave a flick of his toes and slowly propelled himself upwards. He drifted towards the surface. His ascent was so gradual that a large pike swam past his face without a moment's concern. Sam followed it with his eyes, drinking in the merciless curve of its jaw and the rippling scales on its flanks, shimmering like burnished jet stone in the almost total darkness of the reservoir.

As he broke surface and took his first breath of air for over three hours, Sam became aware of their approach. He couldn't tell who was coming, but he knew they were more than one, and he knew, also, with a certainty that chilled his blood, that they were coming for him.

III

Darkness, Fire & Blood

FRAGMENTS OF TIME

He lay on his back on the surface of the water and watched the moon rise. As he lay there, Sam found fragmented images crowding into his head, more vivid than dreams, more real than memory. Some he could control. Others he could not.

Fragments of time. Broken pieces of the past. His developing senses seemed to work in retrospect. His memories were still in shards and slivers, moments and feelings, but each fragment was now sparklingly clear. Things that he had remembered only dimly, now he could see and hear, smell and taste.

He remembered his mother's funeral. Looking down as he walked along the gravelled path at the toes of his new leather shoes. The shoes hurt his feet. A very large lady in black was holding him tightly by the hand.

She seemed as old and as huge and as distant as a mountain. This was Grandma Evans. His father, Llew, looked small and lost in his crumpled black suit, slumped down in his wheelchair, as if it were about to swallow him up. A sickly-sweet scent, that Sam now knew to be alcohol, hung on his father's breath. Looking out of the car window as they drove into the cemetery past row upon row of gravestones, Sam was reminded of a city, a vast and sprawling city of the dead. There was a smell of wood smoke, catching in the back of his throat. Somewhere, someone had a bonfire going. How red and wet the earth was.

But new images came crowding into his head, unbidden, obliterating Sam's memories of the funeral. Stronger than the past, here were visions of the present. A new sense, a new sight, was being revealed to him.

As clear as if it were in front of his eyes, he saw Llew, in the kitchen back at the flat. Llew wheeling himself over to the cupboard. Llew opening the cupboard and lifting out a bottle of spirits, unscrewing the cap, the cap dropping onto the lino-covered floor. Sam saw the bottle cap rolling across the floor, describing a half-circle on the lino before disappearing under the fridge. Sam saw Llew watching the top roll out of sight, then shrugging his shoulders. He saw his father take a long pull from the bottle and gasp and shudder.

Out on the marsh, less than a kilometre away, lying in deep and freezing water, lost, far away, inside his head, Sam watched it all, again and again.

The moonlight glinted on the water. Sam floated, as still and as silent as a decomposing log.

CROSSING THE BRIDGE

Earlier that day, Georgette had returned to the stables and taken the spare keys from the hook on the wall in Norman's office. They were in her hand now, inside her jacket pocket. She was holding them tight. The cold metal dug into the flesh of her palm. It helped distract her from the fear that was gnawing at her insides. She was afraid of the night, afraid to be out here so late, alone, afraid of who or what might be lurking on the marsh.

She walked up the deserted pavement on the road bridge. The bridge crossed the canal and fed onto the flyover, and beneath the flyover were the stables. Cars and lorries thundered by, their occupants all blind to the lone figure of the spindly girl leaning against the concrete barrier and looking down into the canal.

She took the jam jar from her pocket, unscrewed the lid, and tipped the contents, waterweed, dragonfly nymph and all, back into the canal. Looking down into the dark water, she recalled the droning conversation held beneath her window by two lingering drunks just after closing time.

'I wouldn't fish there no more, not for a million quid! Not after what my mate saw. He used to go night fishing. He won't be doing that no more. It's bad enough drinking in this place. That canal gives me the screaming hab-dabs nowadays, I can tell you.'

'What about that kid what's gone missing? You know that Llew, sometimes drinks here, bloke in a wheelchair?'

'Welsh geezer?'

'Yeah, that's him. Well it's his son, the kid that's gone missing. Sam, or Sid or something. They reckon he might be in the water.'

'Drowned?'

'Maybe. Or dumped there after someone did him in.'

'Police'll probably drag the canal sometime soon.'

'Or send down divers, maybe.'

The drunks had wandered off into the night, leaving Georgette sleepless in her bed, staring up at the ceiling.

Now she chewed at her lower lip and moved on,

crossing the water and reaching the damp concrete steps leading down to the marsh and the stables. Leaving the roar of the traffic behind she descended into the still and quiet of the night marsh.

THE ART OF STILLNESS

Sam went back to the tunnel. His nerves were in turmoil and he couldn't stay in the depths of the reservoir any longer. The water had suddenly seemed too cold, too transparent, too liquid an element for him to bear.

Under the embankment, with earth and stone piled above and around him, and the still, shallow muddy pool at his feet, he felt a comforting sense of security. He was safe, hidden away in the dark and the cold where no one would find him.

Or so he hoped. But they were coming for him; he knew that, though who they were he couldn't tell. He had the sensation that some, at least, of those searching for him on the marsh were familiar to him. But he could tell no more than that. His senses were currently dominated by his newly acquired gift of sight. He couldn't switch it off. His mind and all his perceptions were filled with repeating images of his father.

Again and again on an endless loop inside his head he saw the bottle top roll under the cooker and Llew take a swig of drink. But why? The moment seemed utterly insignificant. His dad was getting drunk? So what? It was a common enough occurrence. Though, at first, Sam had the strong impression he was seeing something that was actually happening, now, after endless repeats, he couldn't tell if it was a kind of memory, a scene from the present, or a vision of the future.

Maybe now, back in his tunnel, he could calm his jumbled fears enough to try to make sense of them. He needed to sit awhile in the dark, not moving, his breath still and his heartbeat slowed, and the truth would crystallise and he would understand.

But as he took his accustomed place, seated on the ground, with his back against the brick wall of the tunnel, he saw with a sudden, terrible shock, that he was not alone. There was a figure seated opposite him, a man.

Sam shuddered with startled horror and a rasping cry escaped his lips. His legs jerked spasmodically and his feet churned the water on the tunnel floor. He stared transfixed at this person who had stolen into his sanctuary, somehow unseen and unpredicted, and who was now gazing across at him with intense interest.

Then the man spoke.

'Stillness,' he said. 'Utter stillness. It is an art, is it not? An art that took me many years to learn, and even now my meagre talent is but a fragment of what you have achieved in mere days. The mastery of stillness gives access to the secrets of invisibility, amongst other things. I know you are there. When my presence startled you, for which, by the way, I must offer my sincerest apologies, I saw you clearly enough. But now, you are invisible to me once more.

'No matter. It is enough that I know you are there and listening to me. Allow me to introduce myself. I am Father David Lee. You and I share the same heritage, the same ancestors, though not, I think, the same blood. We both have relatives who were born on the tiny island of Luhngdou in the South China Sea. You know this, yes?'

Sam made no reply. He continued to stare at Father David in shocked surprise.

'There is a mysterious force locked deep in the genetic code of our people, a force for good lying dormant in all but a very few, passed down from mother to son, from father to daughter, generation after generation, until . . .' The priest broke off and took a moment to compose himself before he continued.

'Over the years those driven by ignorance, fear and greed have sought to destroy that force, to root it out and annihilate it.

'They have almost succeeded. It is my belief, Samuel Lim-Evans, that you are the last of the dragon-folk of Luhngdou.'

Sam opened his mouth. He realised then that he hadn't spoken for days. There was a numbness in his throat as he tried to form the words, a choked sensation, as if his voice was a window he couldn't open, a window that had been sealed up, its lock and hinges painted over and over again. He had to force the words out, and they emerged as a slurred and distorted parody of speech that shocked Sam far more than it seemed to affect his visitor.

But for all that, his words were just about intelligible.

'Who are you, and what are you talking about?' he said.

AT THE PERIMETER FENCE

The security lights spilled their harsh glare over the outside paddock and the prefabricated outbuildings of the stables. Georgette undid the padlock and slipped through the gate. She was still fumbling with the chain, trying to refasten the lock, when she heard footsteps. Someone was stumbling through the tussocks of grass beyond the wire fence.

Trembling with alarm, the heavy iron lock and chain slipping through her fingers, she succeeded in locking herself within the confines of the stables. She was in clear view, however, standing by the gate under the blazing security lights. Whoever was out on the marsh was bound to see her.

She jumped as someone called out. There was the hissing ring of the wire as a hand gripped the fence and roughly shook the mesh. A bulky figure was standing pressed up against the stable's perimeter.

'Georgette! All right? It's Aaron. From school. What you doing here?'

Georgette's heart was still pounding in her chest but her shock was now coated with the thick syrup of relief.

'Aaron! You made me jump. I'm just here to take care of the horses.'

'What horses?' Aaron squinted through the wire.

'They're in the stalls, under the flyover. Isn't Adda-Leigh with you?'

Aaron coughed.

'Yeah, well. She was.'

Georgette stared at him through the wire mesh fence. 'Where is she?'

Aaron jerked a thumb over his shoulder, indicating the darkened marsh beyond the security lights.

'What? You left her out there on her own?'

'She's crazy!' Aaron spread his arms. 'And I'm not well, me. I haven't been in school all week. The doctor says I have to take things easy! And besides,' he looked at his watch, 'it's late. Gone midnight. My mum'll kill me when I get home.'

'Where did you leave her?'

'Look, she wouldn't stop! It's dark and it's cold and it's nasty out there. I'd had enough. She made me go through that tunnel under the railway. That place creeps me out! My trainers got filthy. And Sam's not even out there, anyway. He's run away, he's living in a squat or something. I don't blame him. His dad's a right alky!'

Georgette fixed Aaron with a long, cold stare.

'Don't look at me like that!' He flapped his arms at her and backed away from the fence. 'I'm not well. I've had enough! If that silly cow wants to hang out on the marsh in the middle of the night then that's her look-out. It's nothing to do with me. I didn't even want to go in the first place!'

He stumbled away, breaking into a trot as he neared the steps that led up to the pavement. Georgette heard him coughing and his trainers scuffing on the concrete stairs before all sounds of him were lost amongst the background rumble of passing traffic.

She looked out through the wire-mesh fence, straining her eyes to see beyond the pool of light that surrounded the stable yard. Out there the marsh lay hidden in such total darkness she could not tell where the land ended and the night sky began.

THE SWORD AND THE FLAME

'I shared a cell with a monk from Wales once. He taught me to speak his language, and I taught him mine. We told one another stories from our homeland.

'He told me of a Welsh prince who, returning one evening to his camp, was horrified to find his tent in disarray, his baby son missing and his favourite hound lying asleep with its muzzle all stained red with blood. Instantly he drew his sword and killed the dog. He was sure the beast had gone mad and devoured his child.

'But imagine the Prince's feelings when he found that the child was safe, sleeping contentedly beneath the upturned crib, and that a great wolf lay dead, its throat torn out, on the far side of the pavilion. The dog had saved the Prince's child from the wolf, but the prince, believing his hound to be a monster, had killed him.

'That story makes me think of those Westerners who first encountered the secret of Luhngdou Island. They saw what they thought was something monstrous. They brought their fire and their torments and tried to burn it out. But unlike the Welsh prince in my friend's story, they never realised their mistake.

'As you see, I wear the vestments of a priest, and I still consider myself a servant of God, but I have long since parted company from any established church.'

The man stopped speaking. Sam looked at him. He was a small man, of oriental appearance, wearing a black suit and a dog collar. The man sighed.

'I'm sorry. I'm not explaining this very well. Perhaps I should begin by asking you what you know of your ancestry? What you yourself were told about your heritage?'

Sam remained silent.

'Nothing?' the man raised his eyebrows. 'I see. Well, the first Westerners came to the island in the fifteenth century. Amongst their number was a priest called Vitas Jorgsen. Jorgsen was a member of a secret society called the Knights of the Order of the Pursuing Flame. On Luhngdou he discovered temples decorated with images and carvings of a great, coiled dragon. The Knights saw these dragon-temples as proof that the local people worshipped the devil. Jorgsen was joined by other knights of the Order and they fell upon the defenceless citizens of Luhngdou and made a great slaughter amongst them.

'Some survivors fled to the mountains while others opted to convert to the religion of their new over-lords. In time, they too joined in the persecution of those local people who persisted in the older faith. The Knights were convinced that the adherents of the dragon cult possessed the power to turn themselves into fearful serpents. The only way to stop it was to convert them to Christianity, or to subject them to the sword and the purifying flame. Transformations into dragons being first evident in the skin, any islanders suspected of belonging to the cult were regularly skinned alive, or burnt at the stake.'

The small priest broke off again and leaned forward.

'Am I making things any clearer?' he said.

'Go on,' said Sam. His voice echoed around the walls of the tunnel, raw and scared and guttural, like the snuffling half-growl of a frightened beast.

THE MESSAGE

Georgette turned the key in the lock and opened the door that led to the indoor arena and the stalls where the horses were kept. During the day, the large gates were opened up too, but Georgette left these bolted shut.

She closed the door behind her and clicked the latch. Turning on the light she breathed in the rich, warm and comforting smell of hay, manure and the horses themselves.

She walked across to Dandelion's stall and leaned in through the open upper door. The horse lifted his head and whickered a greeting. She stroked his coarse mane and spoke to him softly for a while. Then she turned her back on the stall and took out her mobile phone. She took a deep breath and punched in Adda-Leigh's number.

'Hi, this is Adda-Leigh!' The recorded voice spoke chirpily into her ear. Georgette let out an anguished hiss. The recording continued. 'Why don't you leave me a message and I'll get back to you? Bye!'

'Addie? It's me, Georgette. Call me when you get this message. I've just seen Aaron. Are you okay? If you're on the marsh, head for the stables under the fly-over. I know you didn't think I had the guts to go with you today, but I'm here now, if you need any help. Call me when you get this message.'

Georgette lowered the phone and stood in silence while the light traffic of the early hours rumbled by on the flyover above her head.

THE BADGE

'Where did these beliefs come from, that the island people could turn themselves into dragons? Was it merely superstition and religious intolerance run wild or was there any truth hidden behind that smoke-screen of fear and cruelty?

'The Luhngdonese people were dispersed. Many were hunted down. Some fled the island and settled in distant corners of the world. Others hid themselves closer to home and gave themselves ordinary sounding Chinese or Korean names like Lee and Lim.

'But whether at home or abroad, they were never safe. For although the Knights of the Pursuing Flame had long been outlawed by the Church, the order continued to exist, as a secret society of brutal assassins. Originally consisting only of Europeans, the Knights soon began to recruit from islanders who had turned against their own people. They were determined to exterminate every last surviving member of the dragon cults of Luhngdou and to pursue their ancestors down the ages until none were left. The Order was in possession of certain ancient texts which prophesied that, if they did this, they, or their ancestors, would be rewarded with dominion over all the peoples of the earth.'

The priest fell silent and reached into his jacket pocket. He took out a small package bound with silk, which he unwrapped. He held out his hand. A fire-blackened object lay in his palm. It was a metal badge, scorched by flames. Despite the darkness in the tunnel, Sam's eyes easily picked out the design. A cross with a wreath of flames at its centre, a sword in its upper right quarter and in its lower left, a writhing dragon pierced by a lance.

'This is the badge of the Order of the Knights of the Pursuing Flame.'

'Where did you find it?' Sam asked, his terrible voice catching and trembling as he struggled to form the words.

The priest was silent for a moment. When he spoke, his voice was heavy with regret.

'It was amongst the burnt-out ruins of your grand-parent's restaurant in Wales. Someone in your family must have been an agent of the Knights of the Flame, willing to sacrifice their own life to stamp out the continuation of the dragon line.'

'What are you talking about?'

'I have studied the hidden history of Luhngdou and the Order. I have seen many secret manuscripts, some ancient, some of more recent origin. I have always believed that a chosen few amongst the people of Luhngdou did, truly, become dragons. Now I know that I was right.'

'What are you talking about?' Sam said again. It felt easier the second time, as if his voice had already carved out the words and it was now just a matter of running his tongue around the same chiselled shapes.

Father David returned the badge to his jacket pocket and withdrew another, larger object. He held it up. It was a pocket torch.

'Please,' he said. 'Do you mind?'

Sam said nothing. The priest switched on the torch, filling the tunnel with bright yellow light. He pointed the torch at the expanse of shallow mud-filled water that covered the tunnel floor. The surface of this still pool reflected the light as clearly as a polished mirror.

'Look into the pool,' said Father David. 'Look into the reflection, Sam, and see for yourself.'

ILLUMINATED

Georgette was out at the fence again, scanning the marsh for any sign of Adda-Leigh. The scents and sounds of the horses had not calmed her fears for long. She hadn't been able to stay inside.

But standing out under the stark lights left Georgette feeling horribly exposed. A girl, alone, by the side of the empty marshes, illuminated by the security lights for all to see. Except there was no one there to see her. Was there?

She opened up Norman's office, found the panel of electric switches and turned off the spotlights.

After a few moments of temporary blindness, her eyes became accustomed to the gloomier illumination provided by the streetlights on the flyover and the headlamps of the passing cars.

She went back to the fence. Standing with her fingers gripping the wire mesh, she stared into the gloom, looking for Adda-Leigh, looking for Sam, looking for anyone who might be out there.

Georgette was alone and invisible in the gloom of the stable yard. She had often longed to be somewhere quiet and out of sight where she could try to come to terms with the recent changes in her home life. But now she understood the limitations of that condition. Adda-Leigh had become her friend, and although concern for the horses had brought Georgette to the stables, it was fear for the safety of her friend that had her scanning the darkness of the marsh.

But she saw no one. A keen wind ruffled the grass and whispered through the hawthorn bushes and plucked at the withered tendrils of last summer's brambles.

Georgette looked at her watch. One o'clock. Was Adda-Leigh really still out there? Should she phone her home number to find out? But what if Adda-Leigh had managed to sneak back in without her parents knowing and was peacefully sleeping in her room? Georgette's call would ruin everything.

And yet somehow, Georgette felt sure Adda-Leigh wouldn't leave the marsh until she'd found Sam. Maybe she should call the police? She looked out again over the boggy scrubland just as a car, with its headlights on full beam, drove down the far side of the flyover.

For a brief second, a hunched figure was illuminated in the murky distance, standing at the top of the slope leading down to the path that ran under the railway embankment. It was a man, with a blanket draped around his shoulders. He was holding his arm out straight in front of him. With a jolt of horror, Georgette realised what he was doing. There was a gun in his hand, a revolver. He was taking aim.

The car passed and the scene was plunged into darkness once again.

THE BAREST OF MOMENTS

The torchlight filled the tunnel with yellow light and dancing shadow. The gleaming surface of the water pooled on the tunnel floor showed, in perfect reflection, the brickwork of the roof above.

Father David spread his fingers and gestured towards the water.

'Look!' he said, his voice no more than a whisper. 'See!'

Sam leant forward.

As he leant toward the shining surface to look and to see his own reflection in the still water Sam's mind was suddenly hit by a tempest of images.

He saw Llew, in the flat, the empty bottle lying on its side on the kitchen floor, the wheels of his chair resting in a pool of spilt liquor. He saw an ice-covered bag of chips from the freezer, sagging on the table, thawing quietly. Llew had put the chip pan on the stove, with the gas burner on full. His head was tipped back, his mouth open, his eyes closed. Sam saw that his father was snoring.

And he saw Adda-Leigh picking her way through the marsh grasses and slick patches of mud.

And he saw what she saw too, a man pointing a gun at a grey-haired woman in an anorak. The woman was standing with her back to the gunman, quite unaware of the danger she was in.

These images swirled like a blizzard inside Sam's head as he leant forward to look into the pool of water.

And then it happened. There was the deafening hammer-blow report of a pistol being fired outside the tunnel. Father David turned with a gasp of alarm and the torch fell from his hand. It dropped with a splash into the water.

Sam heard neither the gunshot nor the splash. What he had just seen reflected in the surface of the water had momentarily caused his senses to close down in utter shock and disbelief.

Leaning forward in the tunnel, he had gazed upon his reflection for the first time since he left home over a week ago. He had seen, for the barest of moments, a face twisted and stretched out of all recognition.

His skin was bunched into scaly clumps, in contrasting tones of cool blue-grey with a rust-orange sheen. Although his features were still recognisably human, his cranium seemed to have elongated slightly and his hair had matted into blue-black spines arranged in spiky rows along the top of his head. His jaw jutted forward and, as his mouth dropped open in horror at what he saw, his teeth were revealed, a double row of viciously hooked fangs. But the eyes that looked back at him from this terrible reflection were his own, unaltered, and all the horror and despair of a lost soul trapped inside an endless nightmare could be seen reflected there.

Then Father David dropped the torch into the water and Sam saw no more.

INHUMAN

Georgette saw the flash from the muzzle and heard the blast of the pistol from across the marsh. Then from the same direction, came the sound of a girl, screaming. Hardly knowing what she was doing, she turned and ran back to the arena.

With the door firmly closed behind her, she grasped her mobile in trembling hands and called the police. But as she waited for the emergency services operator to connect her she heard a noise from somewhere outside that turned her blood to ice.

The horses heard it too. Some of them began to kick and stamp in their stalls, whinnying and snorting with fright.

The phone slipped from her fingers and smacked down onto the concrete ramp that led to the exercise yard. The battery burst out of the back of the mobile with the force of the impact and skidded away, disappearing into the sand that covered the floor of the arena.

Georgette had no idea what had made the noise out on the marsh. One thing was certain, however. It wasn't human.

BLIND TERROR

The noise began somewhere in his chest. For a moment Sam didn't realise what it was. It seemed impossible that he was actually responsible for the sound. It rose through him, taking control, taking him over.

It was like vomiting, only twenty times worse and one hundred times more powerful. He opened his mouth to scream and his jaw seemed to stretch far more than was possible, as if his head was trying to turn itself inside out.

The sound was released now. It poured out of him in an ear-splitting, agonised roar that shook the bricks of the tunnel and set the railway lines singing on the track up above.

Father David fell to the ground, his hands clapped over his ears. Sam watched, terrified, as a plume of liquid fire exploded from his own mouth and poured into the pool of water churning at his feet, which instantly began to bubble and boil, filling the tunnel with thick white steam.

Gripped by blind terror he leapt to his feet and ran, scraping his head and neck along the tunnel roof before bursting out into the night.

A mental picture of his own monstrous features span around and around in his head. But somehow, too, he was still aware of Adda-Leigh. She was close by and she was afraid, not of Sam, but of the man with the gun. She had seen him shoot down the grey-haired woman. Now he was pointing the gun at her, pushing her along the path that led to the stables.

'Can't have no witness,' the gunman said, with a twisted smile. 'You shouldn't be here. And when I pull this trigger, you won't be!'

Outside the tunnel, Sam blundered through a fog of confusion and fear. He was running, but he didn't know where. His senses were tangled up. He had momentarily lost the use of his physical eyesight and had nothing but inner sight. He couldn't see where he was going. He was blind but he was still moving with reckless speed, pounding across the uneven ground, his own weight dragging him on, out of control. This turn of speed carried him further and faster than he would have believed possible.

With a thunderous bellow of pain, he smashed into the wire mesh fence surrounding the stables. The fence posts crumpled as if they were made of tin and the wire mesh wrapped itself about him like a giant net. He thrashed his limbs, desperately. At last, he sloughed the shattered remains of the fence from his back and shoulders and stepped out of a circle of twisted iron and torn wire.

He made a loud hissing sound as he gulped down great lungfuls of air and struggled to recover his breath. His vision cleared suddenly. Adda-Leigh and the man with the gun stood before him like a waxwork tableaux. They had reached the outskirts of the stable, heading for the canal. Sam had overtaken them with ease. They gawped up at him as he stood there, swaying, looking down at them both. He had grown taller in the past week.

The man was aiming his gun at Adda-Leigh's head. Sam let out a furious scream. He had no control over what happened next. Another gout of flame was hurled from his mouth, igniting the blanket around the man's neck and the brown leather jacket he had on beneath it. Dropping his gun, the man beat at the flames, shouting in pain and fear.

Sam snatched up the burning man and ran with him. He covered a hundred metres in a matter of seconds and threw him headlong into the canal. The man landed with a splash and a hiss. He surfaced and set up an agonised wailing.

Sam turned away and went back to where he had left Adda-Leigh. She was still there, standing trans-fixed with shock.

She looked up at him and tried to speak. Her mouth opened and closed but no sound came out. Behind her the gates to the indoor arena slowly swung open. A figure on horseback rode out. It was Georgette riding Dandelion.

Sam watched as Georgette rode over to the devas-tated fence. One of the posts was still stuck in the ground, leaning at an angle, the metal torn and twist-ed at its base. Georgette seized it and gave it a yank. With a metallic squeal the post snapped at the base. Georgette lifted the fence post and tucked it beneath her arm, holding it like a lance. She looked straight at Sam and took a firm grip on her makeshift weapon.

Then Sam's vision clouded over again. A series of images ran like wildfire through his mind. With a jolt of horror at his stupidity he suddenly understood that his father was about to die.

THE CHARGE

Georgette listened from behind the paddock gates as Sam destroyed the wire mesh fence. Some of the horses were panicking, rearing and kicking in their stalls. She couldn't bear it. Dandelion was looking at her over the gate of his stall. Georgette ran to him, away from the sounds of destruction out in the yard.

Although his flanks heaved and his eyes rolled with fear, Dandelion allowed her to lead him from his stall. His nerve held and he did not shy.

An old saddle and bridle had been left outside the tack room. Georgette gathered up the heavy leather gear. Dandelion seemed calmed by the familiar routine as Georgette hurriedly strapped on the riding tack.

She led the horse to the outside door, drew back the bolts then gave the gates a push. The gates swung open under their own momentum. Georgette put her foot in the stirrup and swung herself up onto Dandelion's back. Then she gave the reins a flick and walked the horse out to face whatever lay beyond the gates.

When she looked back on the events of this night it would often occur to her that, had she been able to stand the tension and the fear of not knowing what was happening outside, hiding out in the paddock would have been by far the more sensible option. What she actually did could be seen as an act of extreme folly precipitated by her own cowardice. Would it have been braver to remain in hiding? Her understanding of the nature of courage was changed for ever that night.

She rode out and saw Adda-Leigh. And then, through a blur of horror and disbelief, she saw the creature that was standing beside her.

Numbness gripped her then. She acted without any clear thought. A strong impulse to fend off this monstrous thing that was threatening her friend and terrorising the horses led her to take up the broken fence post.

Dandelion shied and snorted with fear but Georgette patted his mane and whispered a wordless something to him and he settled. She urged him forward and he responded with an aggressive stamp of the foot and a harsh whinny. Georgette hefted the fence post into the crook of her elbow and together they charged the beast down.

Later, in countless nightmares, Georgette would relive the jolting, breathless, heaving struggle. She would feel again the jarring impact of the fence post as she jabbed it again and again into the creature's body.

The beast staggered and snarled and bellowed. It flailed its limbs and threw back its head and spat a plume of flame into the air. It clawed at its eyes and Georgette realised then that it couldn't see her. She drew back warily and watched.

Adda-Leigh hadn't moved. She too stared at the monster. Georgette heard her gasp with surprise.

'Oh,' she said, and there was wonder in her voice. 'Oh,' she said again, and this time her voice was filled with sorrow.

THE FIRE AND THE SKY

Llew, head back, snoring. The chip pan on the roaring stove bursting into flames. Llew waking with a gulping snort and spinning his chair wheels in a panic. This was all Sam could see.

He was dimly aware of buffets and blows raining down on his body and he struggled to remain on his feet. But all he could see was his father, a man who had, in his time, delivered lectures on fire safety, now in the grip of drunken panic, forgetting everything, lifting the blazing chip pan, holding it at arm's length, trying to wheel himself, one handed, across the kitchen to the back door. It was a vision that left Sam paralysed with helplessness.

But it was another gout of flame, involuntarily spat out into the night sky, which brought him momentarily to his senses. His attackers had ceased their furious assault. Sam shook his head from side to side vigorously. Dimly, he recognised that an instinctive course of action was about to present itself.

He felt a sudden, inexplicable need to stretch. His spine crackled and a terrible burning sensation shot up and down his back and across his shoulders. The pain was so intense it took his breath away. He stood, swaying on his feet while a silent scream tore at his insides but found no release.

He felt his arms lifting, his shoulders flexing and his elbows pumping in an overpowering reflex over which he could exert no control. At last, the scream that had been welling up inside him burst out of his throat as a high-pitched sustained wail of pure agony. It was accompanied by a shower of cinders that scattered like an exploding firework and hung in the air, glowing blood red against the darkness of the night.

Sam felt a series of agonising jolts and heard an awful crackling, rending sound, which at first he thought must be the fabric of his shirt being torn. But it struck him that he was not wearing any clothes, and that he hadn't, in fact been wearing anything since he first came to stay on the marsh.

The ripping sound continued. It was like a drumstick being slowly torn off a whole roasted turkey. His back felt wet, as if it were running with sweat.

Sam opened his eyes and saw Georgette on her horse and Adda-Leigh on foot, both staring at him with horrified looks. Adda-Leigh took a step towards him and tentatively held out her hand.

Then flames burst across his vision, blinding him to all else.

He saw that Llew had dropped the chip pan and the kitchen was on fire. The upstairs flat was empty. There was no one to raise the alarm. The man in the wheel-chair, his dad, Llew Lim-Evans, was only minutes from certain death.

Sam flexed his shoulder muscles. He felt the rush and rustle of waving grass blades down at his feet as something large swung out at his back and pushed against the air like an oar through water. He let out a cry of shock and surprise as he felt himself lifted up into the night sky.

PANTHER ON THE MARSH

'We're alive,' said Georgette. 'It didn't kill us.'

'Why would he have wanted to kill us?' said Adda-Leigh.

They looked at each other. There was a numbness to their speech and their movements. They were both in the grip of profound shock and their words and actions had become automatic.

There was a shout from the marsh. A small man was struggling across the grass. He was carrying a grey-haired woman draped in his arms. She was wearing a bloodstained anorak.

'The police will be along any minute, I hope,' said Georgette. 'I did call them. I got interrupted. But the gunshot ought to bring them running.'

She was still clutching the iron fence post. Pulling a

face, she threw it down. It hit the ground with a muffled clang. 'Stay and tell them there's a woman who
needs an ambulance out there.' She felt a moment of
surprise at her sudden need to act, to speak, to take
charge.

Adda-Leigh nodded.

Georgette pushed Dandelion into a canter and was
soon beside the couple on the marsh. The small man
had laid his injured companion down on the waterlogged ground.

'Help is on its way,' Georgette said, dismounting.
She stood, holding Dandelion by the bridle, not knowing what to do. 'It's probably best not to move her,' she
said.

The man didn't seem to hear. He bent over the
woman and carefully straightened her glasses. She
smiled, weakly. The man spoke to her.

'I believe the food in the hospital will be very much
to your taste, Mrs Hare. I've heard they serve pud-
dings of a type you're unlikely to have encountered
since your schooldays. Jam roly-poly. Stewed prunes
in pink custard. Jam tart topped with grated coconut.'

'Father, I would like a drink of water, now please
. . .'

'Of course, Mrs Hare . . . Of course, Prudence. As
soon as the doctors say it is okay for you to drink . . .'

The woman smiled again.

'Why Father David,' she said, 'that's the first time you've ever called me by my first name.'

'Call me David. Just David.'

'David. Yes. It's often struck me that it's a bit odd to be calling someone "Father" when they're actually young enough to be your son.'

'I know, I know. Rest now, Prudence. Everything will be all right.'

'That bullet had my name on it, didn't it?'

'Hush, now.'

'But at least I saw him fly, David. We found him didn't we? It's mission accomplished, isn't it?'

'Yes. Yes, it is. We got to him first. And you got me here in one piece. The rest is down to me. You just need to concentrate on getting yourself well again. I will find the boy. Metamorphosis is not yet complete. He needs help. His powers are so great, yet without guidance there's no knowing how they will affect him, how he will ever learn to control them. I just hope I am up to the task.'

'You'll be fine, David, don't worry. We were quite a team, weren't we, you and I?'

'Yes, and we will be again.'

'No. I don't think so. The bullet cut through my spine, David. I'm all broken up inside.'

'Prudence. You are going to get better. You must!'

Tears glistened on the man's cheeks. The woman

coughed, and a thin trickle of blood appeared at the corner of her mouth.

'Look!' she said, suddenly raising her head and staring out into the darkness. 'Look there, up on the railway embankment. The panther. It's here.' And the woman smiled once more. 'I think I'll go with the panther, now, David.'

Georgette scanned along the embankment but could see nothing there. When she looked back the man was holding the woman by the hand but her head had slumped to one side and she lay still.

'She is gone,' the man whispered at last. He lowered his head and wept.

EMERGENCY SERVICES

Sam cleared the canal, but only just. His trailing feet were only centimetres above the surface. Crisp was still treading water and crying out for help. He dived beneath the surface, gibbering with fear, when Sam swooped overhead.

A police car with its blue light flashing came careering across the road bridge as Sam, heading in the opposite direction, frenziedly beating the air with his wings, rose up to pass over the roof of the Ferryman's Arms. He caught the television aerial a glancing blow with his right leg as he flew by, but he didn't slow for a moment.

He hurtled through the air without grace or rhythm but he arrived at the back door of the flat on Dartmead Lane within seconds of leaving the marsh. There was no time to waste.

He looked through the glass in the back door. The kitchen was filled with dark smoke, a swirling black fog in the midst of which glowed ominous patches of bright orange flame. He could see no sign of Llew.

Sam closed off his lungs against the choking fumes. Beating his wings, he hauled himself up and away from the door and then swung back down, letting gravity carry him with all its might, smashing against the pane of glass in the kitchen door.

The glass shattered and the door splintered into matchwood as Sam exploded into the room. Enlivened by the sudden influx of oxygen, the fire leapt up to meet him like an excitable hound welcoming home its owner.

Embraced by flame, his flesh lacerated by shards of glass, Sam sought his father within the inferno. He found him down on the ground, seeking out the last molecules of uncontaminated air, his upturned wheelchair lying across his legs.

Sam threw the chair into the middle of the roaring blaze that had engulfed the kitchen table. He lifted Llew and cradling the now unconscious man in his arms, he blundered out of the kitchen and down the hall to the front door. He aimed a kick and the heavy oak panel split in two. Shielding Llew from the jagged splinters of the shattered door, he carried him outside. Gently, he laid his father down on the rain-damp pavement.

It was only as he straightened that he noticed the smoke rising from the charred skin on his arms. Then he felt the pain. He took a few stumbling steps before his legs buckled beneath him and he slumped to the ground. The pavement was deliciously cold. The last thing he heard before he slipped into unconsciousness was the wailing of sirens as the fire engines turned into Dartmead Lane.

The North East London Gazette

MURDER ON THE MARSHES

Detectives at Glass Street Police Station were today questioning a forty-year-old man in connection with a brutal murder at a local open space. The body of Mrs Prudence Hare was found on the marshes late last night when police responded to an emergency call. She had been shot. Two fourteen-year-old girls and a man in his thirties, said to be a priest, were also taken in for questioning. All were later released.

The suspect was rescued by police from the nearby canal where he had apparently been attempting to escape. A handgun, believed to be the murder weapon, was found on the marsh, several metres beyond the towpath.

The incident has shocked local residents. 'I heard the shot, then a little while later I heard someone splashing around in the canal,' a resident told our reporter. 'When the police fished him out, he was shouting and raving about dragons taking over the country.'

SHADOW OF THE WALL

Sam did not know how long he was lost to oblivion. The pain of his burns nagged at him, trying to rouse him, and slowly built to a pitch where he was forced to open his eyes and shift his position.

He thought at first that he was back in his tunnel on the marsh, but when he raised his head and looked around he saw that he was still laid out where he had fallen, in the shadow of a brick-built garden wall, two doors down from his flat. He could make little sense of the chaos around him. It was only later that he was able to patch together some idea of events from fragments of what he had seen but barely comprehended. The firemen in their bulky uniforms, the hoses and the great jets of water powering into the flat, the flashing lights of the emergency vehicles, the paramedics carefully lifting a stretcher into the back of an ambulance. These memories told him that Llew had, at least, a chance of survival.

Whatever telepathic connection had been established between Sam and his father was broken now. Sam had no way of telling if he'd got to him in time. A second too late and the corrosive fumes within the burning kitchen would have poisoned his lungs and left Llew for dead.

For the moment, Sam had to put all his strength into remaining unseen. The emergency crews were busy with the fire and hadn't noticed him. Instinct had taken over, and his utter stillness rendered him invisible.

But how long could he remain concealed? The nagging pain was a distraction. If he moved, he might be seen. What would happen if he was found and taken to hospital? Would they take him for a victim of terrible burns, as if the heat had melted his clothing into his skin, so it now resembled the hide of a dragon? They might try skin grafts, cutting away his scales, unwittingly behaving like the torturers of the Order in a misguided attempt to save his life.

Fear concentrated his mind and Sam remained unseen, even when a burly fireman tripped over his foot. The man merely cursed and hurried back to his colleagues, unaware that anything out of the ordinary lay hidden by the shadow of the brick wall.

Sam could already feel the charred and blistered outer layer of his hide beginning to heal itself. The lacerations from the broken glass were also closing up and the bruised flesh, where Georgette had hit him with her makeshift lance, was recovering fast.

There was less activity now on Dartmead Lane. Finally, the last of the fire engines drove away, leaving the burnt-out flat, already drenched by fire hoses, wide open to the steady rain.

Sam stayed where he was. More than anything else now, he needed rest. Despite his fears for his father, Sam realised there was nothing more he could do. He had reached him as soon as he could, and he had been alive when Sam carried him out of the flat. Sheer exhaustion buried his remaining worries. Sam closed his eyes and slept.

The Marshside Free Advertiser

FORMER FIREMAN IN RESCUE DRAMA

A former Fire Brigade hero was rescued from a fire at his Dartmead Road flat late on Saturday night. Llew Lim-Evans, 42, whose fourteen-year-old son, Sam, is still on the police missing persons list after disappearing a fortnight ago, was taken to Saint George's Hospital suffering from the effects of smoke inhalation.

Fire fighters discovered Mr Lim-Evans on the pavement outside his burning flat when they arrived to tackle the blaze. It is unclear how the unconscious man, who has been wheelchair bound for some years, was able to escape. Speaking from his hospital bed Mr Lim-Evans told our reporter that he was pulled from the flames by 'an angel'. Evidence suggests that someone did in fact enter the building and drag him to safety though no witnesses to this bold rescue can be found. The fire destroyed both the ground floor and the unoccupied first-floor flat.

NEW WAYS OF LIVING

When Georgette woke up her father was sleeping propped in a chair next to her bed. Although it was long past midday, all was quiet downstairs. After a minute or two, he opened his eyes.

'I closed up the pub for the day,' he said. 'After all that palaver last night down at Glass Street nick I reckon you could do with some peace and quiet. Come downstairs and let me make you some breakfast.'

Georgette was feeling numb. Images from the night before swum in her memory. At the police station, she had tried to tell them about the creature on the marsh but they hadn't understood. Adda-Leigh had simply told them it was another man who had thrown Crisp into the canal. A psychiatrist had been called in to deal with Crisp, who was down in the cells, screaming about dragons. Georgette had been given a cup of sweet tea and she'd been sick twice. She stopped referring to the creature as an 'it' and the police took her statement.

Georgette's father chopped up his fried egg with the edge of his fork.

'If you get worried about the horses you can always tell me, love. I'd have gone down the stables with you, no problem.'

Georgette nodded. Her father wiped the yolk from his plate with a slice of white bread.

'I'm glad you're living here, with me,' he said, quietly. 'I know it's not that great and I'm always behind the bar and that. But I am glad you stayed in London. So . . . I'm thinking of looking for a different job. I mean, you'll be grown up and left home before I know it so I ought to make the most of it while you're around. Meanwhile, there's your mother. Don't you think you ought to go up and visit her sometime?'

'Yeah,' Georgette sighed. There would be time to talk to Adda-Leigh, to find out why she'd lied to the police about the creature on the marsh, time to share their memories, to recover from the trauma of last night together. In the meantime there was still ordinary life to be got used to.

'Yeah, I'll go up and see her for a weekend or something. You don't mind, do you, Dad?'

''Course not. It's a new way of living, that's all. We all have to get on with it.'

MOUNTAIN WOMAN

Water dripped from the charred ceiling. The mains pipe had been damaged in the fire. Wind-borne rain-drops blew in through the gaping doors and windows.

Sam had crawled back into the shelter of the burnt-out flat as soon as he was able. He lay still, nestled amongst the blackened debris on the floor, letting the rank smell of countless carbonised materials drift across his consciousness. Ashes stuck to the puckered skin of his back. Water fell onto his shoulders and his forehead. He let himself swing gently in and out of sleep.

Sam opened his eyes and there was a large woman standing very still in the doorway of the gutted kitchen. She seemed as old and as huge as a mountain.

'Hello, Sammy love,' she said. 'I'm your grand-mother. I came as soon as I could. Got the coach up from Swansea. And I find all this hullabaloo when I get here!'

She tutted softly.

'When I heard there were strangers in Mynnodd asking questions about the old Chinese restaurant I thought, dear me, this sounds like trouble brewing. Still, it sounds as if your renegade priest is on the side of the angels after all.'

The old woman spoke in a soft and melodious whisper, barely any louder than the sound of the water dripping one drop at a time, down onto the floor.

'Your mother told me a bit about her family, about her ancestry. Llew couldn't bear any of that sort of talk, though. Superstitious mumbo-jumbo, he called it. To tell the truth, it frightened him silly.

But it's not just your mother's side of the family that's got all the scale and claw. Why do you think there's a whopping great dragon on the Welsh flag? There are plenty of us Welsh with the spirit of that dragon inside them. What my own grandfather used to call "a touch of the worm in the blood". I know "worm" is a funny kind of word to use, but there you are. It's a name first given by people who were too afraid to say dragon. They tried turning it into something small and wriggly. But a dragon is still a dragon, isn't it, whatever its size?

Well, that's what drove your father out of Wales. He wouldn't stay at any price, and don't let him tell you otherwise. Too much mystery in the valley for the likes of my Llewellyn.'

Grandma Evans shifted her great bulk from foot to foot and glanced up, a little anxiously, at the charred ceiling before continuing.

'Your father is a proud man. Too proud for his own good. After the accident it was ten times worse. He would never come home, not even for a visit. And when poor Suzi passed away, well, he wouldn't let me come up to help the two of you at all. Couldn't bear to have anyone looking after him. Well, he'll have to put up with it now, for a while at least.'

She fell silent again. She sighed and looked around her at the ruined flat.

'Your mother would have told you, Sammy. She would have told you what to expect if she'd been able. She wasn't sure herself, of course. You could have turned out just another carrier, like she was. And what with the way Llew felt about it all, I expect she was going to tell you when you were a bit older but she never got the chance. Her heart was much weaker than she realised, poor thing. I should have told you what I knew myself, I see that now. But, what with all the trouble with your dad and all . . .'

The wind picked up and an ominous creaking from

above caused the old woman to look up at the ceiling once more.

'Listen, Sammy. I'm not sure how safe it is in here, for me or for you. There'll be someone along soon to board this place up, see? I'm heading back to the hospital myself. You don't have to worry about your dad. I'll see he's well looked after. You saved his life, Sammy, and I'll make sure he knows it.

'I'll understand if you want to lie low. You're special now, and a lot of people won't understand the way you've changed. But don't forget your family, Sam. Your dad'll always love you, and you'll always be welcome at my house in Mynnodd.'

Grandma Evans stepped back out of the ruined flat and walked slowly down the path to the gate. Sam barely knew her, but still he wanted to call her back, to move, to hear her quiet, undulating voice, her kind words, to let her see what he had become.

But he stayed hidden amongst the ash and the rain. In spite of all that she'd said, Sam was afraid of how she'd react if he stepped forward out of the shadows of the burnt-out flat and growled out her name. There was only one person for whom Sam was willing to take that risk, and he knew he had to go to her now.

AT THE WINDOW

Sam flew over Marshside. The sky was filled with a pale silver light. Dawn was breaking. A lone car drove down Gunpowder Row, but there was no one walking the streets. Sam wouldn't have cared if there had been. He ignored the instinct to stay out of sight. He had to see Adda-Leigh.

His thoughts must have flown on ahead of him and alerted her because she was already awake and standing at her window when he arrived.

He found a slight updraft, an early-morning thermal stirred into life by the rising sun, and he let himself drift with it, circling slowly until he was level with the first-floor window of the house in Union Road. Despite his size and shape he found he could hang on the air currents as efficiently as a gull or a hawk. He floated just beyond the windowsill and regarded her solemnly.

Adda-Leigh looked into his eyes. She opened the window.

'Hello, boy,' she said softly.

Sam raised one hand. His fingers, elongated to twice the ordinary human size and slate blue in colour, tipped with elegantly curving claws, flexed in a rippling wave.

'I knew it was you. The moment I saw your eyes.' Adda-Leigh sighed. 'I always thought that if I tried to be a good person and I just acted all positive about the things I wanted, then I'd somehow always get my way. But it doesn't work like that. I wanted us to be friends. But I picked the wrong time to get to know you, didn't I?'

Sam inclined his head and Adda-Leigh sighed again.

'Thought so,' she said. 'Just my luck. By the way,' she added, 'you look truly unbelievable. And I'm sure I'll never say that again to anyone and mean it in quite the same way!'

The wind picked up and Sam shifted his wings, riding the swell.

'You have to go, don't you?' Adda-Leigh said.

Sam inclined his head once again. Adda-Leigh reached out and Sam placed his palm gently against hers. Her hand felt as small and as soft and as unlike his own as the underside of a cat's paw. He was a different species now.

He closed his eyes and felt the wind gathering its strength.

'Stay in touch. Call me sometime. You've got my mobile number,' he heard her say before he extended his wings and let the wind take him.

THE STORY BEGINS

Eleven years before . . .

Suzi Lim-Evans is feeding the ducks with her young son, throwing bread into the canal from the footbridge. It is not long since they moved to this part of London, to their new flat in Dartmead Lane.

Llew is at work, on the day shift at the fire station. It is a beautiful spring morning, warm, with a gentle breeze blowing from the marsh. A bumblebee, newly awake from hibernation, drones by. The ducks dabble and splash in the water and quack gently as they feed.

When the bag of breadcrumbs is empty, Suzi and Sam walk over the bridge onto the marsh, hand in hand. Sam stumbles and nearly falls, tripping on the uneven tussocks of grass, but his mother holds onto him and stops him from falling.

'Whoops!' she says. 'Never mind!' And today Sam really doesn't mind. He is comfortable and happy and he has everything he could possibly want.

'Shall I tell you a story, Sam?' says Suzi. Sam nods contentedly. 'I'll tell you a story about a little boy, a little boy who found a magical pearl and the pearl turned him into a big, lovely, wonderful dragon!'

And Sam knows that his happiness is now complete, for this is his favourite story.